BlackBuried Pie

A Black Cat Cafe Cozy Mystery Series

by Lyndsey Cole

CONTENTS

Chapter 1

Annie sighed with satisfaction when the delicious aroma of blackberry pie filled her nose as soon as she entered the Black Cat Café Wednesday morning with Roxy trotting at her side.

Until she saw Leona's angry face.

"Where are the blackberries you were supposed to pick up at Hayworth Farm?" Leona practically spit the words out as she looked at Annie's empty hands. Annie's mother Mia, stood behind Leona with her finger to her lips, shaking her head at Annie to keep silent.

Annie willed herself to stay calm and not take the attitude personally. This Leona was not the Leona Annie was used to. The fun and wild Leona changed the day she revealed to Annie that she was her birth mother and not her aunt. Annie tried to be patient while this new mother-daughter thing sorted itself out.

That and the craziness of the upcoming Fourth of July weekend seemed to be pushing Leona to her limit and her patience was nonexistent.

"I wanted to help you here first. Once the rest of the help comes in, I'll pop over and pick up the blackberries. Okay?"

"I guess so," Leona replied before opening the oven and pulling out a big batch of blueberry muffins.

They worked in silence. Annie filled the pastry case, the breakfast cart, and the coffee cart and Leona filled her already-made crusts with the last of the blackberries from the previous delivery, carefully sliding them into the oven. The oven door closed just before the café door opened with the first customer.

Robbie Benson shuffled into the café, tapping his cane on the hardwood floor as he made his way to the pastry case.

Annie raised her head and frowned. Robbie grinned at Annie, showing where a front tooth was missing and he pointed his gnarled finger at a blackberry pie in the pastry case. "I'll take one of those, sweetheart. I have something big to celebrate today."

Annie felt her blood start to boil as she held the freshly baked blackberry pie in her hand and imagined it smashing into Robbie Benson's wrinkled face. She could almost see the blackberries spraying over his white button down shirt and bits of crust sticking to the few hairs that rimmed his ears. Her hand jerked forward before her brain forced her body under control. Instead, she handed the pie to him over the pastry case. She certainly wasn't *his* sweetheart. No woman in town could tolerate his condescending attitude. The thought made her stomach lurch with disgust.

"Here you go, Robbie. Don't eat it all in one sitting." Or maybe you should and suffer the consequences, she thought behind the fake smile. She watched his hunched over body hobble to the cash register to annoy Mia before leaving the Black Cat Café.

"What is it with that guy?" Annie asked Mia and Leona. "You two grew up with him, didn't you? Has he always been such a negative, angry, little man? I'm surprised he'll even eat blackberries from Peter Hayworth's farm. Those two hate each other."

"He's more the age of the Crowley twins." Leona pointed her finger at Annie and Mia. "Mark my words. He'll eat three quarters of that pie and bring the rest back for a refund saying the berries were too sour!"

Mia laughed. "I hope I'm here when that happens. You'll probably pick him up by his shirt collar and throw him in Heron Lake."

Martha, from the Fabric Stash across the hall from the Black Cat Café, entered with her coffee mug. "Who is Leona going to throw in the lake?"

"Robbie Benson," Annie said in between her laughter.

"That old coot? What did he do now?"

"Nothing in particular. He just rubs us the wrong way," Leona said as she took more pies out of the oven.

"He rubs everyone the wrong way." Martha filled her coffee mug with the new Irish Crème coffee. "I'm completely addicted to this new flavor. I don't know if it's the coffee or the Irish Crème liqueur but I'm in trouble if you have it here every day." She closed her eyes and took a sip. "Can I have a piece of pie? The smell is too good to resist."

Annie cut a big slice for Martha and slid it onto a plate.

Martha took a bite and blackberry juice ran down her chin. "This is heavenly," she said, savoring the tart-but-sweet burst of flavor. "Now, what were we talking about?"

"Robbie Benson."

"Oh yeah." After wiping her chin, she made herself comfortable on a stool at the counter. "I remember him back in grade school. He was a pipsqueak and a bully. Bob and Harry Crowley kept him in his place. I doubt there's any love lost between them over the years."

Leona elbowed Martha. "Did you pick one of those twins yet?"

Martha finished her Irish Crème coffee and used her finger to get every last bit of blackberry juice off her plate. "No need for that! I kind of like them fighting over me. Ever since the Valentine's Day dance, one or the other takes me out for dinner and a movie every week. And I still can't tell them apart." She laughed. "I've agreed to let them both escort me to the barbeque on Friday before the third of July bonfire."

Leona harrumphed. "Escort you? They'll be putting you to work. They've run that chicken barbeque for the last fifty years."

Martha winked. "That's what they think. I'll be teaching them a thing or two, and I made them new aprons for the occasion."

Annie sipped her coffee. "Do they know yet?"

"Nope." Martha giggled.

Bree and Ashley Jordan rushed into the café, putting a stop to their conversation.

Annie was glad that Leona made the decision to hire summer help. Catfish Cove was overrun in the summer months and having two extra pairs of hands made all the difference. The two sisters were as different as night and day. Bree was flirty and great with the customers and Ashley was smart as a whip, especially with numbers.

"Sorry we're late, Leona, I didn't hear my alarm go off," Bree said breathlessly between gasps for breaths of air.

Ashley rolled her eyes. "Out too late again is more likely. I heard you climb in through the window."

Bree shot Ashley a nasty glare as she threw her backpack in the corner behind the counter.

Leona handed each girl an apron. "It will be busy any minute now. Bree, you're working with Annie at the pastry display. Smile at the customers and restock when you have a chance. Ashley, you get the cash register this morning. Both of you will be at the ice cream window when we open it at eleven. Okay?"

Both girls nodded while tying their aprons on.

The café began to fill up with unfamiliar faces, ending the women's gossipy conversation. The breakfast cart with two kinds of granola and several fruit juice choices was mobbed. The coffee cart had a line of people waiting for their morning dose of caffeine. Annie and Bree's hands were kept busy serving blueberry muffins, slices of blackberry pie, scones, cinnamon rolls and every other choice from the pastry case.

"Do you make all these goodies right here in the café?" a friendly voice asked Annie.

"Yes. We get up early to have a good selection fresh from the oven."

"Oh. The smells are fantastic. I can't wait to bite into this slice of blackberry pie." The woman leaned closer and cupped her hand around her mouth. "Is there whipped cream too?"

Annie pointed to the coffee cart. "There should be a bowl of whipped cream on ice with the coffee selections. Let me know if I need to refill it."

The woman thanked Annie and moved along for the next customer to make a choice. Leona was busy grilling breakfast sandwiches and making smoothies. She definitely could use some help.

"Are you all right here by yourself for a while Bree?" Annie asked. "I need to help Leona."

Bree nodded and smiled to the next customer in line.

Leona shooed Annie away, sending her to pick up the blackberries.

Walking to the parking lot, Annie was surprised to see a dark green Subaru parked where her old faithful Saab was supposed to be. That Saab had traveled with Annie for the past ten years and she felt a little guilty with this new vehicle. Her new car had the wrong color, the wrong feel and it always started! Roxy couldn't care less. She jumped into the back seat and made herself comfortable for the ride to Hayworth Fruit Farm.

Annie expected to meet Peter Hayworth, the old farmer who owned Hayworth Fruit Farm, in his barn ready to load her up with the berries. Only problem was, she didn't see him anywhere when she parked next to his tractor. The berries were neatly waiting for her, but no Peter.

She loaded the containers into the back of her car. "Come on Roxy, let's walk out to the fields, maybe he went back out to do some more picking. I want to at least say hi and thank him." She grabbed her camera and followed Roxy's disappearing white blur.

The air hung heavy with humidity. Roxy charged ahead, sniffing all the trails that only her nose could smell. She flushed a partridge out of some bushes and the noise it made startled her. Annie meandered and took some photos for her gallery opening at the end of the summer, then turned left toward Roxy's bark, assuming she was enjoying some belly rubs from Peter in one of the many blackberry rows.

As Annie moved closer, a horrible smell assaulted her senses. What could he be doing out here? Was this a new type of fertilizer for the berry bushes?

Annie turned up between two blackberry rows where she saw Roxy cautiously sniffing something on the ground about fifty feet away. The rotten smell grew as Annie got closer to Roxy. She had her hand over her nose, breathing through her mouth while trying to avoid gagging.

"What did you find? Some poor dead animal?"

Roxy whined. Annie felt her body go cold in the July heat. She closed her eyes and counted to ten, trying to control her gagging reaction before she lurched around and vomited in the mowed grass.

When she let herself open her eyes, nothing had changed. Peter lay face down on the ground with a shovel pushed into the black dirt next to his body. Silence filled her ears. Without thinking, Annie knelt beside Peter and felt for a pulse. Relief flooded her body when she felt a faint beat.

A pathetic meow came from the blackberry bushes. Annie crouched down until she saw the green eyes of an orange tabby cat huddled in the brambles.

"Come on kitty, I won't hurt you," Annie said, trying to coax the cat out. He inched toward her slightly, enough for Annie to grab him by the scruff of his neck. After marking the row where she found Peter, she hurried back to her car with Roxy close at her heals.

Somehow, she managed to find her phone and punch in 911. Her friend, JC, the dispatcher at the police station answered and Annie blurted out that

Peter Hayworth was passed out in his blackberry bushes.

"Calm down Annie. Is anyone else with you?"

"No. Just Roxy and an orange tabby cat."

"What happened?"

"I'm not sure. There's a horrible smell and he's lying on the ground. Maybe he had a heart attack?"

"Wait by your car. Tyler will be there in a few minutes."

Annie kept herself busy patting the cat as she paced in front of the barn. When the sirens got closer, the cat tensed and leaped from Annie's arms, running into the barn and disappearing between some bales of hay.

"I'm sure he knows his way around here," she said to Roxy to keep herself calm.

Tyler Johnson, the police chief of Catfish Cove, screeched to a halt next to Annie's car. An ambulance and several volunteer firemen were right behind him.

"Where's Peter?" Tyler asked Annie.

She waved her hand in the direction where she had found him. "He's on the ground in his blackberry bushes. The ambulance can follow the path at the edge of the field."

"Get in my car and tell me where to go. Roxy can sit in the back."

It took them a few minutes to find the row Annie had marked and she told Tyler to pull in between the blackberry bushes.

"What's that smell?" Tyler asked, wrinkling his nose.

"I don't know."

"There's still a weak pulse," the EMT told Tyler. The ambulance crew worked at the speed of lighting to get Peter on the stretcher and away from the horrible smell.

Chapter 2

Annie was relieved when she finally walked back into the Black Cat Café. She let the delicious, sweet smells settle deep in her lungs, replacing the stink from Hayworth Farm.

Leona glanced at Annie's empty hands. "Where are the berries?"

"In the back of my car. There was an accident. Peter's at the hospital."

"Oh," Leona mumbled before sending Bree out to help Annie.

They piled the blackberry containers on the counter for Leona's waiting pie crusts. The population in Catfish Cove soared with all the summer residents arriving and bringing along every friend and relative to their lakefront homes for the busy Fourth of July weekend.

The summer residents wandered into the Black Cat Café along with tourists coming for the Fourth of July fireworks. Business was booming. Everything Leona could make sold out quickly but the pies were a special favorite since the berries were fresh from the local farm.

Mia efficiently cleared the tables as customers finished and she made friendly conversation with the tourists. Annie marveled at her mother's ability to put people at ease and the wealth of knowledge she sprinkled into her conversations about Catfish Cove. Mia and Leona were as different from each other as two sisters could possibly be.

"They are hard workers for sure. You must be proud of them," Annie overheard Mia say to Stacey Jordan about her two daughters working at the café.

"They can be a handful, especially when it comes to boys." Stacey grimaced. "They always seem to go after the same one and it usually doesn't turn out well for anyone. I'm glad this job is keeping them busy this summer; one less thing for me to worry about while I'm at work."

Mia leaned closer to Stacey. "We have noticed an influx of teenage boys coming to the ice cream window. Now I know why."

Stacey rolled her eyes. "Just be sure to keep Bree on this side of the window. I'm off to my shift for the visiting nurses. Thanks for the coffee." She held her cup up as she walked out the door.

Tyler poked his head into the café. Annie smiled as he walked over. "Peter Hayworth was released from the hospital. He's lucky you found him when you did or he might have been a goner."

"Have you figured out what happened?" Annie asked, worried about what she'd found at his berry farm.

"Apparently he was trying some new type of fertilizer and the fumes knocked him out. You'd think he'd know better after all these years of farming."

Annie put two gooey cinnamon rolls in a bag and handed it to Tyler. "Here's a treat for you. I know these are one of your favorites."

"Thanks. I'll be sure to share them with JC."

Annie put her arms on the top of the pastry case and leaned toward Tyler. "So, everything is good with you two?"

Tyler smiled. "Yup. I'm taking Dylan fishing tomorrow. He's finally taking a shine to me. I think that was the biggest hurdle for JC. Dylan's happiness comes first for her and I totally get that." He headed for the door with the bag held up to his nose.

The lunch mob followed the breakfast crowd without much of a break. All the customers kept the booths and stools inside packed with the overflow headed outside to the tables on the deck overlooking Heron Lake. Books disappeared from the freebrary shelves faster than ever before. Fortunately, Leona had several extra boxes of donated books that hadn't fit before, so if some people didn't follow the rule of taking a book and leaving a book, they could use the ones they still had in the office.

Roxy meandered around the outside tables accepting friendly pats here and there, especially from all the kids excited to see a dog. Annie couldn't have adopted a better dog. Roxy liked everyone and knew enough not to beg for food from the customers sitting outside.

By the time two o'clock rolled around, Annie, Leona and Mia were happy to be able to take a short break.

Annie pulled the door closed. "I'm glad for the business but—"

"But what?" Leona interrupted. "You're not planning to leave now are you?"

Annie was slightly taken aback by Leona's angry tone, the third time in the same day she sounded ready to bite Annie's head off. Annie was seriously thinking about not working at the café once she got her gallery up and running.

"No. I only," she paused, "never mind. I'll start making more granola for tomorrow."

Leona turned the radio on to the oldies station and pulled out bowls to mix up a batch of blueberry muffins. Mia started a big pot of vegetable rice soup before getting out ingredients for Annie's Crazy

Curried Chicken Salad and Chubby Chickpea Salad which were both popular in the summer.

Bree and Ashley managed the ice cream window which had a never ending stream of parents, kids and teenage boys waiting in line. Especially teenage boys. Annie kept one eye on those interactions, understanding Stacey's worries completely.

Leona slid her muffins into the oven and wiped her hands on her apron. "Okay then. I'm heading to Curl Up and Dye for my hair appointment. These will be done in thirty minutes."

Annie raised one eyebrow but held her tongue until Leona was gone. "What's her problem today?" she asked her mother.

Mia laughed. "Today does seem worse than usual. I think she's worried about her date tonight."

"Since when did a date worry Leona?"

"Since she started online dating again. She's been burned before and it's made her a little gun-shy."

"Great. I hope it goes better than the last time. Do you know any details?"

"Only that he's rich and is looking to invest in property here in Catfish Cove." Mia shrugged. "You know how Leona is about this stuff; every time she thinks she has finally found *the one*."

Loud knocking on the locked door interrupted their conversation. Martha was peeking in the window next to the door gesturing for someone to let her in.

Annie pulled the door open. "Where's the fire?"

"Not a fire." Martha gasped for a breath of air, holding one hand on her chest. "Robbie Benson is dead."

Chapter 3

Annie held Martha's arm and helped her to a booth. Mia rushed over with a glass of water as Martha sank onto the red seat. She guzzled the water and sucked in a big breath of air. "Thanks. I couldn't believe my ears when Bob, or maybe it was Harry, called me and gave me the news. I mean," she looked at Annie and Mia with huge round eyes, "you talked to him in here this morning, didn't you?"

"Yes. He treated us to his miserable old self. Do you know what happened? How did he die?" Annie asked, remembering the pie he bought in the morning and a fleeting memory of her desire to smash it into his face.

"Stacey Jordan found him."

Annie glanced to see if Bree or Ashley were listening. The two girls were still swamped with ice cream orders and teenage boys and had no interest in what Martha was talking about.

Martha tapped her fingers on the table. "He's been one of her patients for a while with the visiting nurses program. I guess she found him when she stopped to check his blood sugar."

Mia and Annie slid into the both across from Martha with puzzled expressions.

"He's diabetic. He was dead when she got there." Martha leaned across the booth and whispered. "In my opinion, Catfish Cove is better off without him, and his sister is better off too."

"Doesn't Hazel depend on Robbie for everything?" Mia asked.

"That's what Robbie wanted everyone to think. She never made friends except for Stacey Jordan, but I always wondered if Robbie wanted her to be dependent on him. Someone he could boss around."

Bree appeared at the booth. "Annie? How late do you want us to work?"

"Leona said she wants to keep the ice cream window open until eight tonight and tomorrow and you can have Friday and Saturday nights off."

Bree peeked quickly behind her. "Oh. Well, I was wondering," she said, exaggerating the word wondering and looking everywhere except at Annie, "if I could leave a little early, because, ah, you know, I forgot that I made plans for tonight."

Annie noticed a boy fidgeting outside the French doors with his eyes on Bree. A tall, gangly, dark haired, nervous teenager.

"Sorry, Bree. I need more notice than that. You have a commitment here." Annie remembered Stacey's concern and decided it was better for Bree to be working than out doing who knows what with a boy.

Bree stomped back to the ice cream window.

"What was that all about?" Leona asked, returning from Curl Up and Dye, as she watched the departing Bree.

Annie rolled her eyes. "Bree is such a drama queen."

Mia's mouth twitched slightly at the corner. "Yes, she is. Reminds me of someone I know when she was younger, but I'm not saying any names."

Annie covered her mouth and Leona glared.

"Yeah, well, being tough on her is doing her a favor. I wish someone had given me more guidance," Leona replied.

Mia and Annie both burst out laughing, unable to contain it anymore.

"I hate to burst your bubble, but you never listened to reason," Mia reminded Leona before changing the subject. "Nice hairdo. When's your date showing up?"

"He's supposed to show up at the ice cream window soon." Leona held up a big bag. "I'm going to change."

Mia slid out of the booth. "I think the soup is cooled off now. I'm going to put everything away and make sure we're all set for tomorrow. This will be our busiest weekend of the summer."

Annie held her hand up to get her mother's attention. "Don't forget the ice cream delivery is coming tomorrow morning. Ask the girls to pull out any empty containers before they leave tonight."

"That will go over like a lead balloon. I see Bree is spending more time flirting with that boy that's been hanging around than scooping ice cream. Are you leaving soon?"

"I think I'll stick around to meet this new beau of Leona's. She's acting about as nervous as I've seen her in a long time. How about you Martha?" Annie asked as she stood up and stretched her arms.

"Definitely. I'm free all evening so we can all check him out and make sure Leona isn't making a bad choice."

"Bad choice? Are you three talking about me?" Leona glared at them with her hands on her hips.

Mia smiled. "We're excited to meet your date. That's all."

Leona twirled around. "How do I look? I'm a little nervous."

Martha nodded. "You're beautiful Leona. I wish I could fit into those jeans. Well, I might be able to squeeze this old body into jeans, but I'm not sure anyone would want to look at me. And your white, silk v-neck t-shirt clings to all the right places." She snorted. "I like the red highlights in your hair too, just like Annie's."

"I'm glad Tess decided to stay in town. She's so talented with hair styling." Leona draped her arm around Annie. "Yes, we do look like mother and daughter now, don't we."

"Ms. Robinson?" A deep, husky voice startled the women.

Leona's cheeks had a slight blush when she turned toward the voice. "Mr. Carbone?"

Annie watched the man's eyes travel from Leona's strawberry blond hair with the red highlights down to her heels which made her almost as tall as he was. She saw something in his manner that seemed off, or was she suspicious because Leona met him online?

He held his hand out warmly. "Call me Luke. Pleased to meet you. Leona?"

Leona grasped his hand, at a loss for words.

Martha blurted out, "Introduce us to your sexy friend, Leona."

Luke's lip twitched up at the edge. "Are your friends coming with us to dinner?"

Leona's head swiveled around before settling back on Luke's handsome face. "No. Of course not. Mia, Annie, Martha, this is Luke," she said without taking her eyes off his face.

His eyes twinkled. "Pleased to meet you ladies." He held his arm out for Leona. "Shall we go now? I thought you might like to have a few drinks and dinner at the Fitzwilly Tavern. It was highly recommended when I researched Catfish Cove."

"Yes. That would be perfect."

Leona finally looked at her friends and raised her eyebrows. Martha gave a thumbs up when Luke's head was turned away.

Annie nudged her mother. "Weren't we heading over there too?"

Leona's eyes flared and she said with a steely voice, "You can't leave Bree and Ashley here unsupervised."

"That's too bad. I would love to have all of you join us," Luke offered.

Leona started walking to the door with her arm entwined in Luke's. "As nice as that sounds, they can't leave yet. It will have to be the two of us."

"Maybe another time?" he said over his shoulder as Leona pulled him toward the door.

As soon as Leona and Luke were out the door, Annie burst into fits of laughter. "Did you see her face when we said we were going to the tavern too? It's way too easy to push her buttons."

A scuffle outside on the deck and Roxy's barking drew their attention away from Leona's departing figure.

Annie rushed outside to find Bree's admirer shoving another teenage boy. She pulled them apart. "You both need to leave now or I'll call the police chief and have him give you a lesson in proper etiquette."

Bree watched from the doorway with her hand over her mouth before running after her boyfriend. "Wait Todd. I'm coming with you."

Ashley appeared at Annie's side. "My mom's going to kill her. She's so boy crazy."

Annie put her arm on Ashley's shoulder and walked her back into the café. "Maybe it's better this way. You two sisters didn't seem to enjoy working together. Do you have a friend looking for a job?"

Ashley's face lit up in a huge smile. "Yes. I do. Should I bring her tomorrow?"

Annie wasn't usually the one to make hiring decisions, but with Leona preoccupied with her own possibly budding love life, she nodded to Ashley. "We can give her a try. If she works out well tomorrow, she gets the job. With Leona's approval, of course."

Ashley pumped her fist in the air. "Thank you so much. I know she'll work out fabulously." She moved back to the ice cream window where a line had formed again and worked twice as hard to make up for Bree's absence.

"What was that all about?" Mia asked.

"Teenage drama." Annie rolled her eyes. "Bree ran off with her boyfriend so I told Ashley to bring her friend tomorrow to take Bree's spot."

"I'll stay and help her until we close. You can head home if you want to."

"Thanks, Mom. I am tired." Annie called Roxy and they drove back to her apartment.

"Let's take a short walk on the Lake Trail so I can get some more photos for my gallery opening," Annie said to Roxy.

Roxy new the words 'Lake Trail' and was on her way toward the water by the time Annie retrieved her camera from the passenger seat.

With the sun lower on the horizon, she snapped some interesting photos of the sky over the mountains on the far side of the lake. She was excited to be spending more time with her camera. Her recent investment in the Cove's Corner building with the money she inherited from her biological dad gave her the opportunity to start turning Jake's Clay Design shop into an art gallery. Jake would still sell his pottery in the new gallery when it opened at the end of the summer, but he had no problem giving up the business end of marketing his creations. Thinking about her Fisher Fine Art Gallery made shivers run up her arm, even in the July heat.

When Annie was in front of Mrs. Dodd's lake house, she waved to the figure sitting on the porch. She reminded herself to make time for a visit.

A voice behind Annie caused her to gasp and forget all thoughts of Mrs. Dodd.

"I thought I might find you here."

Chapter 4

Startled from her thoughts, Annie turned to see the handsome face of Jason Hunter. His dark eyes creased at the corners as his mouth turned up into a broad smile. Roxy bounded over with her tail wagging and sat in front of Jason, waiting for a treat that he always carried in his pocket for her.

As soon as Roxy was satisfied, Jason wrapped his arms around Annie. "I've missed you so much. What are you doing out here? I expected to find you in your apartment with some delicious meal cooking on the stove."

"Taking some photos. My opening show is going to be Candid Around Catfish Cove." She looked up into his face. "What do you think?"

"Perfect. The tourists will eat it up." He draped one arm over her shoulder as they headed back toward Cobblestone Cottage, Jason's sprawling lake house with Annie's apartment over the detached garage.

"I didn't expect you until Friday."

With a teasing grin, Jason's eyebrow went up. "Oh? Do you have plans with someone else that I need to be worried about?"

Annie swatted his arm. "Don't be silly. It's a wonderful surprise." She nestled her head comfortably in the crook of his shoulder, inhaling the spicy scent.

"I have more of a surprise too if you care to accompany me into my modest abode."

Annie laughed. "There's not one splinter of modest in your abode. Now my apartment that you so kindly rent to me, that's modest."

"You know you're welcome to move into my not-so-modest abode anytime it suits you," Jason teased while squeezing Annie tighter.

"I like my space with Roxy and Smokey. But thanks for the offer."

It was true, Annie thought to herself, she did prefer to have her own place. Not that spending time with Jason wasn't something she looked forward to and enjoyed more every time she was with him. Their time together was special and she missed him when he was traveling, but she wasn't ready to give up her own space. Yet.

Annie untangled herself from Jason's arm. "I'll be over in a few minutes after I check on Smokey. The poor guy probably thinks he's been abandoned, although he is quite happy with the kitty door you let me install for him. I imagine he's terrorizing all the chipmunks that try to come up on the deck."

With her eyes focused on her mail, Annie sifted through the pile before throwing the envelopes on the table. The kitty door opened and closed and she felt Smokey rubbing against her bare legs. His purring intensified as he twisted between her feet.

Bending down, Annie picked Smokey up, cuddling him tightly. "What have you been up to today? Anything interesting?" She buried her nose in his soft fur. "You smell like grass and leaves."

In reply, he head butted her cheek before squirming to get down and walking to his food bowl, tail straight up.

"You certainly have me well trained," Annie said as she dumped some dry morsels into his bowl on her way to take a quick shower and get out of her work clothes. Less than ten minutes later, changed into ivory capris, an emerald green t-shirt and the silver strawberry necklace that Jason gave her for Valentine's Day, Annie smiled at her reflection in the mirror. Tossing her strawberry blond curls, she said, "See if you can resist this, Jason Hunter."

From the corner of her eye, Annie spotted a book on the floor by the kitty door. "I wonder where this came from," she said to Roxy and Smokey as she picked it up and flipped it over in her hands.

"Nothing I've seen before." She flipped the cover open and saw her name scrawled in red ink. *Annie, Oliver knows what happened.* "Oliver? Who's Oliver? What does Oliver know?" She stared at the words as the hairs on her arms stood up. Who stuck this book through the cat door? Annie tossed the book onto her coffee table, determined to put it out of her mind for the rest of the night. "Come on Roxy. Let's see what surprise Jason has for us."

They went down the stairs, two at a time, and walked across the driveway to the main house. Without knocking, Annie let herself in with Roxy at her heels. The table to her left was set for two with a candle in the center and a loose bouquet of blue hydrangeas in a glass bowl. Annie tilted her head back as she sniffed the delicious scent of something in the oven.

Jason already had two glasses of wine poured. "Here you go," he said, handing a glass to Annie. He took a sip, watching her. "I like it."

Annie realized he wasn't referring to the wine. She liked the tingling sensation traveling up her spine from his eyes on her.

"You are a sight for sore eyes. You get more beautiful every time I go away. What's your secret?"

Annie grinned. "Well, you know, if I tell you, it wouldn't be a secret anymore, now, would it?"

Jason picked up a tray with crackers, cheese, hummus and baby carrots. "Let's sit on the porch until dinner is ready. You can carry the bottle of wine."

"Something smells delicious. Have you finally learned how to cook?"

"You know my secret. I'm very good at popping frozen meals into the oven. And unless you have a better idea, we're having eggplant parmesan, garlic bread and a salad."

"That sounds like Leona's signature go-to meal. You two are always scheming behind my back." Annie made herself comfortable on a wicker swing with a view of the lake and helped herself to some horseradish cheddar cheese on a wheat cracker.

"How are you two getting along, if you don't mind my asking?" Jason sat next to Annie and gently pushed the swing back and forth.

"It's complicated. At first, when she told me she's my birth mom and not my aunt, it was like a big weight was off my shoulders. I was relieved to know the truth." Annie turned to look directly into Jason's understanding eyes. "But then she tried to be my mom, and, well, my mom is Mia. I don't want to be between my mom and her sister. I'm sick of that part of our relationship."

Annie took a long sip of her wine. Jason placed his hand on her thigh. "I'm sorry. Finding the truth quite often solves one issue, but can create new ones. Just be yourself. Leona has to figure out her new role."

"But that's the problem. I don't want her to have a new role. I want us to have the same carefree fun relationship we used to have. I'm twenty nine. She can't start over like I'm her little girl now."

The oven timer interrupted their conversation and Jason stood up. "Be patient. She'll work it out."

Annie frowned but tried to shake off the bad mood as she followed Jason into the kitchen. She knew he was right, he usually had a good sense about people.

"This isn't exactly a summer meal, but it's all I could manage to finagle out of Leona."

Annie inhaled deeply. "The garlic and oregano are making my mouth water. Dish it out before I faint from starvation."

Holding the food from Annie, Jason teased, "That would give me an excuse to catch you in my arms."

"I'm not planning to eat and run," Annie replied with a sly glance from the corner of her eyes.

Jason carried the eggplant parmesan to the table and pulled a chair out for Annie. "Good to know."

After Jason lit the candle, he held his wine glass up. "Cheers," he said as he clinked Annie's glass and settled comfortably into his chair. "I'm glad to be home. With you."

Jason served Annie a portion of the eggplant. She helped herself to a big serving of the salad which was loaded with tomatoes, cucumbers, shredded carrots, avocados and feta cheese, with a tangy orange dressing drizzled over the top. "Leona didn't make the salad too, did she?"

"No. I can handle salads. Actually, it's about my favorite thing to make. So, tell me what I've missed around here."

Annie set her fork down and broke off a big chunk of the garlic bread. "Robbie Benson is dead."

Jason's eyebrows shot up, almost to his hairline. "When? How?"

Annie shrugged. "I don't have many details. Martha told me he died today. She heard about it from one of the Crowley twins. Stacey Jordan found him when she went for a home visit."

"Interesting."

"What do you know about that nasty little man?"

Jason chuckled. "Don't mince your words. What did he ever do to you?"

"Nothing, really. He's just rude and condescending when he comes into the café." She stabbed a cherry tomato with her fork.

"I suppose he would be. Interacting with women isn't his strong point."

"And everyone knows how he treats his sister. So, what do you know about him?"

"He has a piece of valuable land that several people have been trying to get their hands on."

Annie's fork stopped half way to her mouth. "Valuable enough for someone to murder him?"

Chapter 5

"Murder? You didn't say anything about murder."

"You're right. I'm speculating. I didn't want to think about this tonight, but, well—"

"What is it Annie?" Jason asked with concern in his voice.

"It's something I found in my apartment."

"And?"

"Someone put a book through Smokey's cat door with a message inside. The message doesn't make any sense to me, but the idea that somehow it's connected to Robbie's death popped into my head." Her fork clicked on her plate as she got back to eating.

"What was the message?" Jason wiped his mouth with his napkin.

"*Annie, Oliver knows what happened.* Do you know an Oliver in town?"

Jason shook his head. "It could be a coincidence. Can you talk to Tyler about it? See if he'll give you any information?"

"I suppose so. Maybe tomorrow. I don't want to bother him tonight about what might just be a wild goose chase. It's Dylan's ninth birthday and JC told me they were taking him out for miniature golf and burgers." Annie refilled her wine glass.

"Fair enough. Too be continued tomorrow then. How is that relationship going?" His eyes twinkled. "As long as Tyler and JC are involved, I don't have to worry about you and Tyler renewing your old love affair."

Annie grinned but didn't give Jason any reply.

Jason finished his eggplant parmesan. As Annie reached for more garlic bread he reminded her, "Make sure you leave room for dessert."

"Are you implying I should watch my weight?"

Annie watched a slight blush creep up Jason's neck. "No, don't put words in my mouth. You're perfect just the way you are."

"I guess I shouldn't eat this second piece of bread." Annie grinned. "What did you make?"

"Well, I can't exactly take credit for it."

"Right. Leona made it. Let me guess. Blackberry pie?"

"How did you know?"

"We've been making them all week. And I picked up another order of blackberries from Peter's farm this morning."

"How is Peter?" Jason asked after stacking the dishes to bring to the kitchen. "I don't know how he manages that big farm."

"Good question. Going to his farm was an interesting twist in my day." Annie carried the salad bowl to the kitchen counter.

Jason returned with the blackberry pie, placing it on the table. "Don't tell me he's dead too?"

"No, at least he wasn't dead when they put him in the ambulance this morning. And I heard he was released from the hospital." Annie scooped vanilla ice cream onto the piece of pie Jason served her. "I found him, well, actually, Roxy found him passed out in one of the blackberry rows. There was a terrible smell."

"This pie is fantastic," Jason said between bites, apparently more interested in dessert than Peter's problems. "Tart and sweet with a light flaky crust."

"They are selling like hot cakes at the moment. I'm not sure we'll be able to keep up with the orders. Especially if Peter doesn't get more blackberries picked."

"Doesn't he have any help?"

"He does, but if he's not well enough to oversee what's going on, the work might not get done."

The candle flickered as Jason got up from the table and turned his iPod to a romantic mix of music.

"Shall we sit on the porch and watch the stars?"

Annie followed Jason to the porch swing with a big smile on her face.

***

Annie woke up when Roxy jumped off the bed and she tensed when she heard Roxy's deep throaty growl. A soft thud came from the main part of her apartment, followed by a rustling noise. Her heart raced. Then silence.

Annie quietly slid out from under her cotton blanket, grabbing her flashlight as an afterthought, which could work as a weapon if needed.

She stood silently behind her bedroom door for what felt like several minutes, listening to the early morning sounds. A few birds sang, a branch tapped against the house from the breeze and the sound of tires crunching on the driveway faded and disappeared. With her heart pounding in her chest, she forced herself to breathe in and out until it calmed to a normal beat. Roxy stood guard between Annie and the closed door.

Finally, she cautiously opened her bedroom door. At first, nothing seemed different. As she entered the room and got a clear view of the big front window to the left of her front door, she saw a book on the floor, about a foot inside the cat door. The hairs on her arms prickled up. The first book that she found the day before still sat innocently on her coffee table.

Annie stared at the book as if it might disintegrate if she stared at it long enough. Roxy sniffed it and poked it with her paw, then walked away disinterested.

Taking a deep breath, Annie picked up the book and opened the cover. *Annie, check the trash*, was written in red ink.

She compared the writing from the two messages and decided it had to be the same person. Who was sending her messages and what did they mean? She checked her trash which was empty, so whose trash was the message referring to?

Smokey let himself out through the cat door. The noise of the flap swinging closed gave her goosebumps with the memory of the sound when the book was pushed through.

With a sigh, she filled Smokey's water and food bowl and picked up her new bag. Martha had started making the cutest quilted bags and Annie couldn't resist buying the one covered with black cats. Black cats were sleeping or jumping and even stretching on the back, and the front had one big curled up black cat on a big pocket. It reminded her of Smokey when he made himself comfortable on the windowsill of her big window overlooking Heron Lake. He always had one eye open and his tail twitched when a bird landed on the bird feeder.

"Okay Roxy, ready to roll?" Annie asked her dog a half hour later. She dropped the two books into her bag and slipped her camera strap over her shoulder.

Roxy sat by the front door, waiting patiently for Annie to clip on the leash.

"I should take lessons from you on how to be patient." Annie laughed as she stroked the soft white fur on Roxy's head. "Come on Roxy. We may as well head to the café and get a jumpstart on the day."

She picked up Roxy's leash and left her apartment. A quick glance at Jason's dark house, and a small smile at the memory of the evening before, was all the time she allowed herself before driving down the hill into Catfish Cove. She looked in awe at the sliver of light and pink glow beginning to peek above the mountains.

Annie pulled to the side of the road to enjoy the silence and the beauty before getting out and snapping several photos for the grand opening of her Fisher Fine Art Gallery.

The squeal of tires taking the corner near Annie made her jump out of the way as Leona's yellow mustang sped by. The top was down and Leona's hair sailed behind her unsmiling face. Annie stared in disbelief at the reckless driving and the lack of acknowledgement from Leona.

Ten minutes later, when Annie walked into the Black Cat Café, Leona had the oldie station blaring and she seemed like her old self. Almost. Annie turned the radio down, prompting a glare from Leona.

"How was your date with Luke?" Annie asked, ignoring the angry stare.

Leona shrugged. "Okay, I guess. Not sure I'll see him again." She pulled cinnamon rolls out of the oven and set them on a rack to cool.

Annie poured two cups of coffee, bringing them to the counter and sliding one toward Leona. "Nothing better than coffee with one of your cinnamon rolls straight out of the oven. Bring a couple over and take a break."

After Leona sat down on the stool next to Annie, they ate in silence side by side.

"Gonna share any more details?" Annie finally broke the silence. "He acted like the perfect gentleman yesterday." That was true she thought to herself. Too perfect, but that was her opinion.

Leona swiveled ninety degrees so she faced Annie. "Yeah, he is. Almost too perfect. Handsome, polite, thoughtful, and he has a boatload of money."

Annie laughed. "What's wrong with that?"

"No one is perfect. He has to have flaws, but he hides them so well he doesn't seem real." She shook her head. "I want to like him, but I'm afraid he's got a motive for being in town and I don't want him to break my heart." She covered Annie's hand with hers.

"You don't have to fall head over heels in love with him after one date. Have a good time and see what happens." She smiled to herself about how they both came to the same conclusion about Luke.

Leona hugged Annie. "How did you become so wise? You must have gotten that from Mia, because there's not one shred of common sense in my body. Don't ever change. I thought I was supposed to be giving you advice, not the other way around."

Annie drained her coffee. "Is that what's been bothering you lately? Feeling like you have to be the mature one in the crowd?" She hoped she didn't touch a nerve.

Leona spun back toward the counter. "I guess so. I thought I had to start being a better role model."

"Don't try to change. I love you for who you are, not who you think you should be."

"Okay." Leona slid off the stool, pulling Annie with her. She twirled her around and they kicked up their heels to the music.

"That's more like it, Leona. I need your spontaneous energy, not a serious unhappy bore."

"I was a bore for the last few months?"

"Uh huh," Annie teased.

Danny Davis poked his head around the café door. "Too early for my coffee and blueberry muffin?" He slipped his Red Sox baseball cap into the back pocket of his khaki shorts.

Leona linked her arm in Danny's and pulled him to the counter. "Sit down, I'll get it for you. I need you to make me some more of those beautiful hexagonal picnic tables for the deck. Everyone wants to sit outside in the nice weather."

Danny smiled. "I have a couple made already. I thought you might be needing them."

Leona kissed Danny on the cheek. "What would I do without you?"

"Did you hear about Robbie Benson?" Danny asked.

"Yeah. Can't say we're too broken up about it." Leona brought him his coffee and a big blueberry muffin with extra streusel on top.

"Did you hear the police suspect murder?" Danny said before stuffing his face with muffin. "Possibly Stacey Jordan."

Chapter 6

"Murder?" Leona sputtered.

"Well. I guess it's more like the death hasn't been ruled from natural causes yet," Danny explained.

Annie filled the granola containers and moved the breakfast cart into place. "Stacey Jordan? Her daughters work here. I heard she found the body, why is she a suspect?"

Danny wiped some crumbs from his mouth with the back of his hand. "That's all I heard from Bob Crowley." He slid off the stool and started to walk toward the door. "Do you want me to bring the picnic tables over this morning?"

"The sooner the better. Customers will be coming in soon," Leona replied.

Luke Carbone brushed by Danny, nearly knocking into him. "There you are Leona. Why'd you rush out so fast this morning?"

Annie couldn't miss the glare Danny gave Luke as he turned around to observe this intruder.

"I have a business to run. Maybe you missed that part of the conversation last night while you were busy talking about yourself," Leona replied as she bustled around the kitchen getting organized for smoothie and breakfast sandwich orders.

"Slow down, babe, don't get your panties in a twist. I thought you were having fun last night."

Leona slammed a container of yogurt on the counter. "Don't call me babe."

Danny grabbed Luke's arm. "Maybe you should leave. Leona's kind of busy."

Luke looked Danny up and down as if he was something that should have been thrown out with the trash. "Get your hand off me. Who are you?"

"It's time to leave." Danny repeated in a quiet but menacing tone.

Luke jerked away from Danny and started to walk toward Leona. Before anything came out of his mouth, Danny had Luke's arm twisted up behind his back and was escorting him out of the café. "You don't listen too good, do ya?"

Leona watched with her mouth hanging open. Annie put her arm around Leona's waist. "Looks like Danny's got your back. He can read people, and my guess is he doesn't think much of Mr. Fancy-Pants Luke Carbone. Oh. I almost forgot. We have a new worker starting today," Annie told Leona, hoping to get her mind off of Luke and Danny.

"Oh?"

Annie filled Leona in on the drama with Bree. "We can't let Bree keep the job if she's so irresponsible. I told Ashley to bring her friend."

Mia arrived at the same time as the ice cream delivery man and opened the door for him. He pushed his hand-cart into the café. "Where do you want this stuff?"

Leona motioned for him to bring it to the freezer. "Everything goes in here for now and we'll stock the window freezer as needed." Mia helped to unload the hand-cart while Leona wrote a check for the ice cream.

The morning rush of customers started to stream in for their coffee, pastries and a view of the lake. By late morning, Ashley and her friend walked into the café, laughing and playfully knocking into each. Bree followed with an embarrassed look on her face. She sidled up to Leona. "Are you really going to fire me?"

Leona put her hands on her hips. "What you did yesterday is unacceptable but I'm willing to give you another chance. I'll give you the benefit of the doubt that it was an error of judgment and you learned your lesson."

Bree's smile spread from ear to ear. She elbowed Ashley. "See, I told you I didn't lose my job."

Leona took Bree by the arm and pulled her away from Ashley and the new girl. "Don't even think like that when you are in this café. You treat everyone with respect. Customers, and especially your sister. Do you understand?"

Bree nodded, her face turning bright red.

"You can work at the pastry counter." Leona walked away to meet the new girl.

"Annie asked me to bring in my friend today. This is Kristen," Ashley said.

"Great. You two can get the ice cream freezer stocked. There's a new delivery of ice cream in the big freezer. Any questions?"

Ashley shook her head. "We can manage that. Thank you."

Annie was happy to hear that drama was sorted out. At least for the moment.

Danny was outside setting up two new picnic tables by the time customers started moving to the deck for seating. Annie smiled and felt her heart beat a bit faster when she noticed Jason helping Danny. He was always ready to lend a hand to anyone in need, even when it put his life in danger. She shivered in the July heat at the memory of Jason rescuing Tess when she fell through the ice last February. She thought she might never see Jason again on that cold dark night.

Leona went out on the deck to direct the placement of the tables and to bring out new red umbrellas.

Bree gently elbowed Annie and whispered, "My mom is talking to you."

Startled, Annie pulled her eyes away from Jason to see Stacey Jordan standing at the pastry counter. "Annie, can I talk to you for a minute?"

Annie followed Stacey outside away from all the people. "Leona didn't fire Bree if that's what you're here about."

"Fire Bree? Why would she fire Bree?"

Oops, Annie thought. Apparently, Stacey hadn't heard about the boy drama yesterday. "Just a misunderstanding."

Stacey was staring out over the lake with something on her mind. "Oh, good. I'm not here about my girls." Her clear blue eyes stared at Annie. "I think I'm in trouble. Will you help me?"

Annie placed her hand on Stacey's arm. "What kind of trouble?"

Stacey looked around before answering. "You heard about Robbie Benson?"

Annie nodded.

She sucked in a deep breath of air and exhaled before continuing. "He's a diabetic and I was the visiting nurse scheduled to visit him yesterday to check his blood sugar."

Annie waited for Stacey to continue.

"It's a routine kind of thing, shouldn't take long. I like when I get the visit so I can say hi to Robbie's sister, Hazel. We've been friends ever since elementary school."

Jason approached from behind Stacey and put his arm around Annie's shoulder. "Fancy meeting you here. Are you on a break? Can I get you some lemonade or something?"

Annie hesitated. "Sure. Get one for Stacey too." Annie lowered her voice and said to Stacey, "Maybe this isn't the best time or place to discuss this. Once the lunch rush is over, I'll try to get away. Can I meet you somewhere?"

"Never mind. I shouldn't be bothering you with my problems." Stacey started to walk away.

"Wait Stacey. I do want to help. Three o'clock at the town green?"

Stacey nodded. "I'll be there."

Jason carefully made his way back to Annie while balancing three glasses of lemonade. "Where's Stacey?"

"She had to get back to work." Annie took one of the glasses and gulped down the cool drink. "I promised to meet her later."

"Sit down with me for a minute," Jason said. "I ran into Tyler on my way here and told him about the book you found in your apartment."

Annie rested her chin in the palm of her hand. "I got another one early this morning. It was creepy. Roxy heard the noise and woke me up but I never saw anyone, just another book on the floor stuffed through the cat door."

Jason took Annie's hand. "I don't like the sound of this. What did this one say?"

"I'll show you." Annie went inside and returned with her bag. She pulled out the two books and handed them to Jason. "The one on top is the first one."

Jason opened the cover and read the message. He put the second book on the table next to the first one and studied the words. *Annie, Oliver knows what happened. Annie, check the trash*. His eyes met Annie's. "It looks like the same person wrote both the messages."

"Yeah, that's what I thought too, but neither message makes any sense to me."

Chapter 7

Leona motioned for Annie to hurry back inside.

"The café is swamped. I'll talk to you later," Annie told Jason as she slid the two books into her bag which was hanging from the back of her chair.

A hand touched Annie on her shoulder as she stood up. "Annie?"

"Peter. How are you?" She studied the kind face of Peter Hayworth.

"Fine, thanks to you. I'm not sure what would have happened if you didn't find me yesterday when you did."

"Actually, it was Roxy who tracked you down."

Peter looked around the bustling deck. "Where is that amazing dog of yours? I owe her a big treat the next time you stop by." As if on cue, Roxy appeared and stuck her nose in Peter's hand. He knelt down to embrace the dog.

"I have to get back to work but I'll stop by the farm later. I'm sure Leona will be needing more blackberries. Come inside and I'll send you home with a pie. That will give you a good shot of energy to get through the rest of the day."

"Just bring it when you visit. I have a couple of errands before I head back to the farm. My kids are visiting for the holiday weekend so I'll be around all afternoon. I stopped in here first to let you know I'm back to normal, thanks to your quick actions."

When Annie finally pushed her way into the café, she couldn't help but notice the long line waiting for breakfast orders. Leona's clenched jaw also provided a good indication of her mood.

"Go out and get a breath of fresh air. I'll take over the grill."

Leona visibly relaxed. "Thanks. The tourists shouldn't be getting under my skin. I think it has something to do with Luke's visit this morning. What was all that with Danny?"

Annie looked at Leona out of the corner of her eye as she flipped the egg and sausage sandwich. "Are you serious? You haven't figured out that Danny has a crush on you?"

Leona's mouth fell open and a slight blush crept up into her face. "We're good friends. I never imagined it was more than that."

"Why do you think he comes into the café every morning? It's not to see me or Mia." Annie piled home fries next to the sandwich and handed the plate to the waiting customer.

"What should I do?" Leona poured a yogurt, banana and strawberry breakfast smoothie into a tall glass, stuck in a sprig of fresh mint and handed it to the customer.

Annie's hands kept busy, frying eggs and home fries. "Think carefully before you do anything. Danny's a great guy in many ways. What you see is what you get. He has some baggage, and at this point he knows you like him as a friend. Don't lead him on unless you mean it or you'll destroy him."

Leona nodded. "I'm going outside for a few minutes. You okay with this?" She swept her arm around the filled café.

"Yeah. Tell Mia to help me, and Ashley can hop between the cash register and the ice cream window."

Morning merged into the lunch crowd without skipping a beat. There was a steady stream of tourists stocking up on delicious pastries, blackberry pies and books from the freebrary. Annie smiled to herself every time she saw someone beam with excitement after finding an author or title on one of the shelves.

Bree, Ashley and Kristen kept themselves busy and even looked ahead for ways to help out. At least while they were in the café they seemed to have gotten the message to put their petty differences aside.

As three o'clock approached, Annie told Leona she had to leave. Mia and Leona were busy making pies and pastries for the next day and Annie had refilled the granola containers and made a new batch of her lunch salads. She searched for her bag on her way out but it wasn't where she usually left it. She smacked herself on her forehead when she pictured her bag hanging on the back of one of the outside chairs.

"Darn it. I've lost my bag," she told her mother. "At least my camera is in here where it's supposed to be, but now I'll have to cancel my credit card and get a new license if it doesn't turn up."

"Don't do anything until you have a good look around. Maybe someone moved it."

Annie called Roxy and searched on the deck. Something black caught her eye near the wooden trash can. She picked up her wallet and was relieved to find all her items still inside, including forty five dollars. Why would someone leave money and take the bag? What else was in there, she wondered.

"Come on Roxy. We need to hustle over to the green to find Stacey."

Main Street was teeming with tourists for the Fourth of July weekend. It was good for all the local businesses but Annie preferred the quieter times. Heron Lake was a beautiful place in the summertime and, of course, all the second-home owners thought the same thing. With so many activities scheduled for Friday and Saturday, the town was crawling with year-round residents, summer home residents and visitors looking for a good celebration.

As Annie got closer to the green, she saw Stacey pacing in front of the gazebo. Annie waved but Stacey was checking her watch and didn't see Annie until she crossed the street and stepped onto the green.

"There you are," Stacey said. "I was worried you changed your mind and decided not to come."

"I wouldn't do that." Annie patted Stacey's arm.

"Of course not, but you might have been too busy." She scribbled her phone number on the back of a business card. "Here, this is my personal cell phone number. You might as well have it in case you need to get in touch with me."

Annie cocked her head and tucked the card into her pocket without looking at it. "What's gotten you so jumpy?"

Stacey sat on one of the benches. "When I got to Robbie's house, he was already unconscious. I called the ambulance but it was too late by the time it got to his house."

"That's not your fault."

Stacey's face relaxed slightly. "Are you sure?" She clutched Annie's arm. "The police won't think it's my fault?"

"What did you do?" Annie asked.

Stacey didn't meet Annie's gaze. "I didn't do anything. It's strange. The room felt different somehow. Like someone else had been there. What do you know about Robbie?"

"Not much, but I don't like him," Annie answered.

"No one did. I'm friends with his sister, Hazel. Not close friends, but I've known her ever since we were kids. She was a shy thing back then and, well, I always felt a little sorry for her; stuck with Robbie for an older brother. She's a writer and sometimes I wonder if her fantasy world is more real to her than the world around her."

Annie nodded, wondering where this was all headed.

Stacey abruptly stood up. "You helped Leona when she was arrested for murder last Valentine's Day. Will you help me if it comes to that?"

Annie kept her voice calm. "Listen, Stacey, I think you're jumping to conclusions. Maybe he died of natural causes."

Stacey shook her head and whispered. "I think Hazel might have done it. She told me she wished he was dead many times. Have you read any of her books?"

"No."

"They're all murders. And the real killer always gets away by carefully planting evidence to incriminate someone else."

"You think she would actually recreate one of her stories?"

"I think it's possible. That's why I'm so scared. I've got two teenage daughters. I can't go to jail. There's no one else to take care of them. My whole career would be ruined if the police even suspect me of murder. Who would hire me to do home visits with that on my record?"

"I'll help you," Annie told Stacey at the same time she asked herself what the heck she was getting involved in.

Chapter 8

Stacey hugged Annie. "Thank you. I have to get back to work. Call me if you think of any questions." She jogged to her car and sped away.

Annie stuck her hand into her pocket and felt the business card Stacey gave her. Pulling it out, she flipped it over and read Stacey's cell number, written in red ink. Annie's blood ran cold. That's what was in her bag—the books. Did someone steal them or just throw them away and take her bag?

"What are you doing here Annie?"

Startled from her thoughts, Annie recognized Tyler's deep voice.

"Are you all right? Your face is as pale as a ghost."

Annie composed herself as much as possible before answering Tyler. "I was talking to Stacey Jordan."

Tyler's eyebrow rose. "I didn't know you two were friends."

Annie sat on the bench where Stacey had been a few short minutes ago. "More like acquaintances, and her girls work at the café. She's having some trouble keeping her older daughter, Bree, out of trouble with the teenage boys." Not a lie, even if it wasn't what they were actually discussing. Annie hoped that explanation would satisfy Tyler.

Tyler nodded. "Did she say anything to you about Robbie Benson?"

Annie paused, knowing she couldn't lie to Tyler. He knew her too well. "How was miniature golf with JC and Dylan last night?"

Tyler laughed. "We had a great time. Dylan hit the holes like a pro. I think he's got some serious golfing in his future. I promised to take him fishing later." He sat down next to Annie. "Stacey did tell you something, didn't she?"

Annie nodded. "She's petrified she'll be accused of something she didn't do." Annie turned to face Tyler. "She's a single mom. She's afraid she might lose her job."

Tyler leaned back with his arms behind his head and his legs stretched out in front. "She should be worried. Robbie died from an overdose of insulin."

"Has that information been released?"

"Of course. Do you think I give you some special pre-info access?" he teased. "The new reporter for the Catfish Cove Chronicle hounded me all morning until I had the confirmed cause of death and gave her a statement."

"Amber Taylor? Martha's granddaughter?"

Tyler nodded. "Yup. There's not one shy bone in her body and she doesn't give up until she gets answers. I suspect she'll be moving on to something bigger once she has some experience on her resume."

They sat in silence for several minutes before Tyler asked Annie a question. "Jason told me you found a book in your apartment. When are you planning to fill me in?"

"Books. There's been two now."

"And?"

"And I lost them. Or someone deliberately stole my bag with the books inside."

"So someone stuffed a couple of books through your cat door. Everyone knows you love books, maybe they were a gift?"

"An odd gift since each book had a message written to me on the inside cover."

Tyler sat up straight. "What did the messages say?"

"The first message was, *Annie, Oliver knows what happened* and the second message said *Annie, check the trash.*"

"Who's Oliver?"

Annie held both palms up. "Beats me. The messages make no sense."

"Anything else you noticed?"

Annie hesitated. "The messages were written in red ink."

"Lots of people could have a red pen."

"That's true." She turned the business card over showing Tyler the phone number written in red ink. "Stacey gave me this. I'm hoping it's a coincidence."

Tyler stood up. "Be careful Annie. Somehow you manage to get pulled into other people's problems. Let me handle this, okay?"

"Of course, Tyler. Why would I get involved?" Why indeed, she thought. Not like she had a choice when information was dumped in her lap.

Annie watched as Tyler headed to his cruiser. She wanted to stay out of the drama but she also wanted to help Stacey if she was in any trouble. Who else did Stacey have to turn to? She would keep her eyes and ears open at the least.

"Come on Roxy. I promised Peter a blackberry pie today."

Annie parked in front of Peter's barn next to several other cars. As soon as she slid out of her car, she heard Peter's booming voice.

"Annie. I'm glad you brought your hero with you." He knelt down and wrapped his arms around Roxy's wiggling body when she ran to him. She even honored him with a big lick up the side of his face.

Annie smiled. Peter lavished more attention on Roxy than he did on most people. "I brought you the pie I promised."

"Good. Good. Do you have time to come in for some tea with me?" He cupped his hand around one side of his mouth. "My son and daughter are here, all worried about me, and I could use a distraction from them."

"Sounds wonderful. I haven't seen your kids in a long time. They probably don't even remember me."

"I always expected Kirk to be my partner on the farm but he doesn't like to get his hands dirty, and Emily was too much of a girly girl to take all the chores seriously." Peter held the kitchen door open for Annie and Roxy. "Emily's two kids will love Roxy."

Sure enough, as soon as those words were out of Peter's mouth, a boy about five years old followed by a chubby three year old with two pigtails coming out the sides of her head, rushed into the kitchen. They stopped abruptly then squealed with delight at the sight of Roxy.

"Grandpa, grandpa," the small boy shouted. "Can we pet the doggie?"

Peter's daughter poked her head around the kitchen door. "What's all the excitement?"

Before she had a chance to ask if Roxy was kid friendly or not, the two children were all over her. Emily's hand flew to her mouth and she moved quickly to grab her children but Roxy stood patiently with her tail wagging.

Annie saw the panicked expression on Emily's face so she knelt down next to Roxy and the two kids. Talking to the children, but also for Emily's benefit, Annie introduced the kids to Roxy and explained how to be gentle and the best places to pat her.

"We don't have a pet," Emily sputtered as she watched the interaction. "They love your dog. Maybe I'll think about adopting a puppy for them."

"If you make that decision, I have a good friend who runs an animal shelter here in town. It's were Roxy came from. I could help you pick out a suitable puppy."

The two kids started to jump up and down. Apparently, the little boy heard every word and he wasn't planning to let his mother forget what she said.

"Okay, everyone. Annie brought a delicious blackberry pie from the Black Cat Café. It's made with our own blackberries. I'm putting on a pot for tea and we can sit down and visit for a bit." Peter filled his kettle and turned the stove on. "Emily, show Annie out to the living room."

"Let me help you, Peter," Annie offered.

Emily was already gone with Roxy and the kids trailing behind her.

"It's a whirlwind when they're visiting," Peter whispered. "Here are plates and forks, if you can carry that out with the pie. I'll be out with the tea pot and cups. You don't mind, do you?"

"Not at all. What's your son's name again?"

"Kirk. And I'd better warn you. He'll bore you with his opinion that I'm too old to still be running this farm, especially after what happened yesterday."

Annie chuckled. "Thanks for the warning."

As Annie walked into the sunny living room, she was happy to see Roxy lying on the rug with the kids scratching her tummy and squealing with delight when Roxy's leg twitched in the air.

"Shall I put all this on the coffee table?" she asked Emily.

"Yeah, sorry." Emily snatched the papers and kids' toys to clear a space for the pie and plates.

Kirk was studying some ledgers at an old roll top desk. "Hello Kirk. I'm Annie Fisher. I'm not sure if you remember me."

Kirk finally tore his eyes away from his papers to acknowledge Annie. "Are you the one who found Dad yesterday?"

Annie nodded, catching the frown on Kirk's face.

"Thank you for that. I wish he would come to his senses and sell this farm. If you hadn't found him when you did, well, who knows what might have happened to him."

Annie sat in a wing back chair. "I understand your concern, but isn't it important that your dad is happy doing what he's doing?"

"Annie, that's what I keep telling Kirk." Peter set the tray with tea next to the pie. "Now, let's help ourselves to this blackberry pie and vanilla ice cream. Come on kids. I brought treats for Roxy too. You can each give her one of these dog bones. Annie told me it was Roxy that saved me."

Kirk turned his chair around facing the others. "Do you think Hazel will still sell the land to that condo developer now that Robbie's dead?"

A shadow crossed Peter's face. "Time will tell."

Chapter 9

Peter and Kirk argued over the future of Hayworth Farm which made Annie uncomfortable. At her first chance, she offered to take the kids for a walk with Roxy. Emily sighed a grateful thanks for the break and Annie happily herded the kids out the door.

She grabbed her camera, never missing an opportunity for some candid photos, knowing the kids would be perfect subjects in the berry rows.

Logan ran ahead following Roxy, and Ariel stuck her little hand into Annie's. She stopped every few feet to examine a rock or pick a blade of grass to show Annie. Once they found a thornless blackberry bush loaded with berries, Ariel let go of Annie's hand to fill her mouth with juicy blackberries. Roxy stayed close to Annie, and Logan never strayed more than a few feet from the dog.

Annie snapped photos of the two kids eating berries and she even caught Roxy daintily nibbling berries for herself. Kids outside, exploring and having fun, made for interesting photo opportunities and a new idea for another show. After the kids' faces were stained purple from the berries, Annie got them headed back toward the house.

"Can you and Roxy come back and play with us again?" Logan asked Annie with his big brown eyes filled with hope.

She rubbed his head. "How long will you be staying here on the farm?"

"We're staying for the fireworks. I love it here. Grandpa usually takes me in the tractor and I help him move the bucket up and down."

"That sounds like fun. I'll tell you what, if I have a chance, I'll bring Roxy back and we'll take another walk."

"Yippee!"

Logan ran to the house with Ariel trying to keep up but she fell and skinned her knee on a rock. Annie picked up the screaming girl who wrapped her arms around Annie's neck and buried her wet face against Annie's chest. She sobbed uncontrollably the rest of the way to the house. After a kiss from her mom and a fancy band aid, the scrape was forgotten.

Peter accompanied Annie out to her car. "Sorry for Kirk's sullen attitude. He's never been able to understand what I love about the land. Logan is the one I have to keep everything for. He loves it here."

Annie nodded. "Yes. He told me and I promised to come back and take them for another walk. Let Emily know that Roxy and I will be in the dog parade on

Saturday and the kids can help me if she says it's okay."

"Great idea. I'm sure she'll be all for that."

Annie paused with her hand on the door handle. "By the way, I forgot to ask you. What happened yesterday?" She was curious if his story varied from what Tyler told her.

"I'm trying some new fertilizer on a few bushes. It was an experimental sample and I didn't realize how strong the fumes would be. I guess the smell overpowered me."

Annie dug the toe of her sneaker in the dirt. "What's going to happen with Robbie's land now?"

"That's the million dollar question, I suppose. Hazel is tough to talk to, living in that fantasy world of hers. It's anyone's guess what she'll do without Robbie bullying her around."

"I've heard the land is valuable. Do you think she'll sell it?"

Peter shrugged. "Probably, but I hope it isn't to that sleazy developer."

Peter's foreman arrived on the tractor pulling a trailer filled with containers of blackberries.

"Perfect timing. I'll buy another load of blackberries for the café while I'm here."

Peter and the foreman loaded up Annie's car. Roxy jumped into the back seat and they were on their way. When Annie pulled out of Peter's driveway, she decided to head down the road to Robbie Benson's house before heading home. Since she was so close she wanted to pop in to see Hazel to give her condolences, at least that's what she told herself she was doing.

Annie saw the Benson's white farmhouse set back from the road when she turned into the driveway. A fancy black car was parked at the side of the house and Annie pulled her Subaru in next to it. When she slid out of the driver's seat, she heard someone pounding on the front door.

"Hazel. I know you're in there. You have to talk to me sooner or later."

Annie hesitated, wondering who was yelling for Hazel. As she took a few steps closer, a face turned in her direction.

"Hi Annie. Any idea where Hazel might be?" Luke Carbone asked in a sugary voice.

She felt her skin prickle at his sudden change of tone. What was he doing here?

"No. I was nearby and dropped in to check on her. Why are you here?"

His eyes darkened. "Don't start in on me. I have every right to be here. Robbie and I had an agreement and I want to make sure Hazel is going to honor it."

"You're not giving her any time to grieve, are you?" Annie bristled at his attitude. "What was this agreement?"

Luke walked past Annie to his car, ignoring her question. "Tell Hazel I'll be back. I intend to own this land no matter what it takes."

Annie's mouth fell open as she watched the dust fly up behind his disappearing car.

The sound of a door opening behind Annie made her look back toward the house. Hazel Benson stood on the front step staring beyond Annie.

"Good. He's gone. Would you like to come in?" Hazel asked in a voice so quiet Annie barely heard her.

Annie stood for a few seconds, wondering what she was thinking coming here alone. This place gave her the creeps. "Do you mind if my dog comes with me?"

A small smile broke the corner of Hazel's mouth. "That's fine." She disappeared inside leaving the door open where she had just been.

By the time Annie and Roxy walked inside, Annie heard water running and the clink of glass to her right. She followed the sound, stepping into a bright kitchen.

As she looked around, Annie was surprised to see a kitchen straight out of the fifties. Everything was spotless and tidy but obviously had never been updated over the years. Roxy's toenails clicked on the pale green vinyl floor. Hazel stood in front of gleaming white metal cabinets. She motioned for Annie to sit at the small white table piled high with stacks of books, probably the newest items in the kitchen.

"Would you like a glass of water?" Hazel asked as she put two glasses on the table.

Roxy sat next to Annie, leaning on her leg. "Thank you. I was at Peter Hayworth's farm and decided to stop in to see how you're doing. It must be quite a shock for you."

Hazel sipped her water, staring at Annie with unwavering eyes. "He was a bully my whole life. Someone did me a huge favor."

One hand went to Annie's mouth and the other settled on Roxy's head. Her gaze left Hazel's piercing stare. "You think it was murder?"

"The police chief stopped in earlier after he got the autopsy report. He said it was an insulin overdose."

"Maybe Robbie injected himself? Made a mistake?"

"Maybe, but he hated needles and rarely injected the insulin himself. I gave him his shot before I got ready to go out for a walk. Before Stacey Jordan arrived."

A small piece of the mystery fell into place adding to what Stacey told Annie. "Do you think Stacey gave him another shot? Couldn't it be an accident?"

Hazel shrugged. "I suppose so. It's a moot point now. He's dead and I finally have my freedom."

Annie's head was swirling. Hazel didn't show one tiny bit of remorse or sadness. How could Hazel be so cold-hearted about her brother's death?

A beautiful orange cat with green eyes jumped into Hazel's lap, keeping her eyes on Roxy the whole time. Annie thought it looked like the cat she pulled from the blackberry bush when she found Peter unconscious.

Hazel stroked the cat and she settled in her lap, purring contentedly. "Where have you been?"

Annie set her glass on the table, getting ready to leave. Hazel seemed to have floated off into her own world.

"He was arguing with someone."

"Excuse me?" Annie was startled by Hazel's words.

"Robbie. He was arguing with someone before he died."

"Do you know who it was?"

"It sounded like Peter. I heard him say, *'Did she sign it yet?'* Then I left when I heard the door slam."

"Where did you go?"

"I hate confrontation so I went for a walk in the fields. That's why I wasn't here when Stacey came."

"What do you know about Luke Carbone? He told me he had some sort of agreement with Robbie about the land."

"Robbie was planning to sell all our land to Luke for a condo development even though he knew I didn't agree with the plan." She continued to stroke the cat. "Robbie didn't care what I wanted."

"What will you do now?"

"Keep it of course. Robbie couldn't have died at a better time. He was going to sign the papers yesterday. That's probably why he bought the blackberry pie. Too bad he never got to celebrate with a piece. It was his favorite."

Chapter 10

Annie's blood ran cold. Hazel sat so calmly talking about her brother's death and eating pie. The sound of a clock tick-tocking in the background made her dizzy.

"Who knew about his plans?"

"I don't know, Robbie probably blabbed it to everyone that would listen to him."

Annie stood up and took her glass to the sink. "Thanks for the water. I've taken up enough of your time. I'll let myself out."

"I like your dog."

"Roxy?"

"Yes. She's well behaved. I would like to get a dog now. Robbie would never let me have one. Could you help me find one like yours?"

"I guess so. Have you ever been to the Second Chance Animal Shelter? That's where Roxy came from."

"No. Will you take me?"

"Now?"

"If you don't mind."

"Well, okay. It's almost closing time but you could take a look."

There was nothing normal about Hazel, Annie realized. She was more like a child than a middle aged woman. Was she capable of murdering her brother? If she did murder him, she had plenty of good reasons. Maybe she could plead insanity.

They walked out to Annie's car. "Do you want to follow me?"

"How?"

"Don't you have a car?"

"I suppose Robbie's car is mine now but I don't know how to drive. I get around with my bike."

"All right then, hop in." What am I getting myself into, Annie wondered, as Hazel walked to her car.

Hazel sat staring out the window, humming. Annie decided that Hazel must be used to spending hours on end by herself.

"Stacey told me you're an author."

"Yes."

"I'd like to read one of your books if you have extra copies."

"Okay."

Annie left it at that. It was pointless to try to engage her in a conversation. Hazel offered information when she was ready.

"Here we are. Roxy can stay in the car."

Annie opened the door to the shelter and let Hazel enter first. Karen's head popped up from the mountain of papers on her desk.

"Annie. How nice to see you. Where's Roxy?"

"She's waiting in the car. This is Hazel Benson. She's thinking about adopting a dog."

Hazel interrupted. "One like Roxy."

Karen waved her hand toward the door to the back room. "You know your way around, Annie. Go on in and take a look."

Hazel walked from one kennel to the next, starting on the left and stopping to study each dog with her head tilted sideways. When she got halfway back up the right side, she stopped and pointed. "That's the one."

Annie looked at the small brown dog with sad eyes. She didn't jump around and bark like all the others, she sat and the tip of her tail wagged a tiny bit. Her brown eyes were irresistible.

Hazel pulled the information card out of the slot. "Her name is Zoe. She's perfect."

"Don't you want to take her out of the kennel and see how she behaves?"

"Can I do that?"

"Sure. I'll slip a leash on her and we'll take her outside."

Zoe calmly trotted from the kennel and waited for Annie to attach the leash. "Here you go." Annie handed the leash to Hazel and led the way outside.

Hazel walked around the fenced yard with Zoe at her side. After she finished one loop, she stopped next to Annie with a big smile on her face. "Can I bring her home?"

"Let's go talk to Karen." Annie wasn't sure it was a good idea, but then again, maybe no one else would come in to adopt Zoe.

Annie explained the situation to Karen who agreed to let Hazel adopt Zoe with the condition that Annie help Hazel get all the necessary supplies she would need for Zoe.

Hazel picked Zoe up and carried her out to the car, keeping her in her lap. Annie stopped at the Black Cat Café to unload the blackberries before going to the farm store for dog food, a bed, a collar, leash and a couple of toys for Zoe.

"Okay then, I'll bring you and Zoe home now."

Out of the blue, Hazel said, "I think that nasty man killed Robbie."

Annie had almost forgotten about the murder. Being with Hazel was filled with surprises and this latest statement brought her back full circle. "What man?"

"The man that was pounding on the door just before you arrived. The man who wants my land," she answered, never taking her eyes from the passing scenery.

"Do you mean Luke Carbone?" Annie glanced sideways at Hazel.

Hazel nodded.

"Do you think that's who Robbie was arguing with yesterday morning?"

"He stopped by almost every day but I never actually saw him yesterday."

"Why would he kill Robbie if Robbie was planning to sell him the land? Now he has to deal with you, and you don't want to sell."

"Robbie needed me to sign the papers too. We owned the land together. I refused to sign."

"That still doesn't make any sense to me. If he was planning to kill anyone, wouldn't it be easier to kill you? Get you out of the way?" Annie turned into Hazel's driveway.

"That would be too obvious. Mr. Carbone probably assumed I would have to sell the land without Robbie around to take care of me. He must have thought I would be desperate for money."

"I didn't think of that. How will you support yourself?"

Hazel turned her head to face Annie. "My books. I don't need to sell the land. Robbie always resented the fact that I was supporting us. He wanted his own money."

Annie was stunned by this newest revelation.

"He wanted to control me but he could never stop my writing or the income would end." Hazel laughed.

Annie stopped in front of Hazel's house next to a red Honda. "Were you expecting someone?"

A frown appeared on Hazel's face. "You need to leave."

"Not yet. I promised Karen I'd help you get Zoe settled. That's why she let you bring her home today."

Annie slid out her side of the car and let Roxy jump out of the back seat. Hazel sat in the car stroking Zoe who was wiggling and whining to get out and play with Roxy.

Annie walked around the car and opened the door. "What's the matter? Is there someone here you're afraid of?"

Hazel shook her head. The sound of a door opening made Annie turn around to see a twentyish year old woman standing on the front step. She had a big smile, a long brown braid of hair and blue eyes that pierced straight into Annie. The face seemed familiar.

"Come on Hazel, at least let Zoe out. I'm bringing the food and bed inside."

Hazel grabbed Annie's wrist allowing Zoe to wiggle free and she dashed around the yard with Roxy. In a voice barely audible, Hazel said, "That's my daughter, Jillian."

"Oh. Is it a problem that she's here?"

"No. I guess not anymore. I forgot for a second that Robbie isn't around to keep her away now. That's how he tried to put pressure on me to sign the sale papers. Sign or never see Jillian again." Hazel finally stood up.

Annie tried to read the expression on Hazel's face. "Can I meet her?"

By then, Jillian was approaching the car. "Mom, are you all right?"

Hazel nodded. "You heard about Robbie, then?"

"That's why I'm here. He can't keep us apart anymore."

Annie held her hand out to Jillian. "Hi, my name is Annie Fisher." Looking from Jillian to Hazel she saw the same piercing blue eyes. Eyes that gave the impression of seeing more than you could imagine.

Zoe and Roxy skidded to a halt to sniff Jillian's hand. "And who are these beauties?"

Hazel was still tongue tied so Annie introduced Roxy and explained how Hazel had just adopted Zoe from the animal shelter.

"Why am I not surprised that the first thing you did is get a dog?" Jillian said, clapping her hands together. "Robbie will be rolling over in his grave." Jillian's face turned serious. "I suppose he isn't even buried yet, is he?"

Hazel shook her head. She put her arm around Jillian's waist. "Let's go inside and get Zoe settled so Annie can go home. I've already taken up way too much of her time."

Annie trailed behind the mother and daughter with a million questions swirling in her head. Questions she couldn't ask. Not yet.

Chapter 11

The drive back to Annie's apartment gave her time to digest the events of the last few hours. Hazel had handed several books to Annie on her way out the door. Mysteries written by Summer Spring, her pen name. Annie wondered if the books would reveal anything about Hazel's life.

Lights were on in Jason's house which brought a smile to Annie's lips. It was a treat to pull in and know someone was there looking forward to seeing her, probably even worrying about her.

She let herself in without knocking, hoping he had something planned for dinner. Soft jazz music was playing in the background and she could see the back of Jason's head through the living room windows overlooking the porch.

Annie tiptoed quietly and peeked around the corner where he was sitting and reading. She gently covered his eyes with her hands. "Guess who?"

Jason's warm fingers softly felt her hands and traveled up her bare arms. "Sarah?"

Annie jerked her hands away. "Who's Sarah?"

Jason started to laugh as he pulled Annie into his lap. "Just teasing. Where have you been? I was just about to call out the cavalry to track you down."

"Well," Annie settled comfortably into Jason's lap, "I had an interesting afternoon talking to Stacey Jordan, Tyler, Peter Hayworth and Hazel Benson."

"I'm not sure I will like the sound of where those conversations went. I hope it had nothing to do with Robbie Benson's death."

"Maybe a tiny bit." She leaned over and kissed his neck.

"Let's get something to eat before you share all that information with me. How about a pizza and beer at the Fitzwilly Tavern?"

"I like the sound of that. I'll need fifteen minutes to shower, change and feed Roxy and Smokey."

Jason pushed the button on his watch. "Not one second longer." He tried to swat her as she hustled through the door but his hand only met air.

When Annie took her stairs down two at a time, cleaned up and in comfortable clothes, Jason was leaning against his car keeping an eye on his watch. The buzzer went off exactly when Annie's foot hit the bottom step. "Not bad," he commented with a grin. "Very efficient, but I think your shirt is on inside-out."

Annie looked down. "No it's not."

Jason grinned his handsome grin. "But your hair is still wet."

"It will dry, and with this July humidity the curls will be unmanageable." She ran her fingers through her hair, trying to crunch it into some sort of order.

Fitzwilly's was crowded so they put their pizza order in and carried a couple of beers outside, finding one last empty table.

Annie sank down with a sigh. "It feels good to sit down and relax. It's been an interesting day, to say the least. Do you want to hear the short version?"

Jason nodded and tasted his beer. "Do I have a choice?"

She shared the important parts of each conversation with Jason as he sat quietly waiting for her to finish. When she reached the part where she found out about Jillian, Annie hesitated.

"Go on, don't leave anything out. It's probably the best part," Jason said.

Annie leaned as close to Jason as she could and lowered her voice. "Hazel has a daughter named Jillian and Robbie wouldn't let them visit each other."

Jason sat back. "That complicates the situation. Who do you think killed Robbie?"

Annie shook her head. "There's plenty of people that will benefit from his death, but Hazel benefits the most. She gets to keep her land, get out from under the tyranny of her brother, and her daughter can live with her." Annie sipped her beer. "She never showed any surprise or even a hint of sadness that Robbie is dead. It was weird."

"What about Luke Carbone?"

"Do you think killing someone and no guarantee that Hazel would ever sign the papers would be worth the risk of losing everything if he gets caught?"

"What about Jillian?"

"She was friendly and relaxed. If she's the killer because she wants to be in her mother's life, she loses that if she's caught."

"Annie, people don't kill someone expecting to get caught. They want something so badly, they think they'll get away with it."

"I suppose your right."

The waitress set a big pizza between Jason and Annie. "Here ya go. One apple cheddar pizza with caramelized onions and walnuts. Enjoy. It's my favorite."

They each slid a piece onto their plate and waited for it to cool down.

Annie felt a hand on her shoulder. "Guess what I found today." Martha pulled up a chair and joined them without waiting for an invitation.

"The bag I bought with the cats on it?" Annie asked hopefully, remembering her missing bag.

"Yeah. Someone found it next to a trash can and saw my label on the inside so she returned it to me. You need to take better care of your stuff, dear. I was afraid you didn't like it but didn't want to tell me." Martha's mouth pouted. "Mind if I have a piece of this pizza? The smell is making me drool."

Jason slid the plate toward Martha. "Help yourself."

After taking a small nibble from the edge of the slice of pizza, Annie said, "Don't be ridiculous. I love that bag. Was there anything inside?"

"No, it was empty. Sorry. Did you lose anything important?"

"Maybe."

Martha took a big bite. "This is delicious. I never had pizza without tomato sauce. Who knew it would be so awesome?" She took a sip from Annie's beer. "How did Leona's date go with that handsome guy?"

Jason asked the waitress to bring another beer so Martha could finish Annie's.

"Not very well. He showed up at the café this morning and made the mistake of calling Leona, babe."

Martha snickered. "I wish I was there to see that. Did he leave with a black eye?"

"No, closer to a broken arm. Danny escorted him out of the café with his arm twisted behind his back." Annie caught a piece of cheese that was hanging off the side of her pizza. "I think Luke is up to no good here in town.

"That's what Harry thinks too," Martha said matter-of-factly. "He's been trying to buy Robbie Benson's land."

Annie thanked the waitress for the new beer. "Where does Harry get his information about Robbie Benson?"

"He's friends with Peter Hayworth. And Peter was fit to be tied about Robbie selling to a developer. It's all he's been talking to Bob and Harry about for weeks. I suppose he'll be happy about this latest development."

Annie stared at Martha gobbling down her pizza. "Do you think Peter could have killed Robbie?"

Martha stopped mid-chew for a few seconds before swallowing. "It never crossed my mind. Peter is too nice of a guy to be a murderer. Right?"

"Maybe he went to Robbie's house to try to talk him out of selling the land, they argued, Peter saw the insulin and injected Robbie, then passed out in his fields from the fertilizer fumes on the way back to his house."

Jason and Martha stared at Annie.

"Are you serious?" Jason asked.

"Hazel heard someone in the room with Robbie before he died and she said it sounded like Peter."

Martha stood up from the table, knocking her chair over backwards into the customer sitting behind her. "I need to talk to Bob and Harry. Find out what else they know." She didn't even adjust her chair before scurrying back to her car.

"You've done it now, Annie."

"What do you mean?"

He finished the last of the beer in his mug and leaned close to her. "You started a rumor about Peter being the murderer."

"He was in the house."

"Did Hazel see him?"

"Well, no, she heard him."

"Maybe it was someone else."

Annie's hand flew to her mouth. "It sounded so neat and tidy. And believable."

Jason covered her hand with his. "I know you're only trying to help, but that's why it's better to leave this to the police. They gather all the facts before jumping to conclusions. Now, how about some dessert?"

Annie's face softened slightly. "What's your recommendation?"

Jason whispered to the waitress. "You'll have to be patient. Something I know you struggle with."

She took a deep lung-filling breath. "Thanks for the reminder."

When the waitress returned, Jason and Annie were laughing and holding hands across the small table.

"I hate to interrupt but I've got your dessert," the waitress said as she placed a huge bowl in front of Annie filled with blackberry ice cream with hot fudge sauce and whipped cream on top with fresh blackberries sprinkled over the cream.

"I can't eat all this," she said with her eyebrows raised in shock.

The waitress stuck a second long handled spoon on Jason's side of the sundae. "This one is to share." She winked at Jason before moving on to another table.

Chapter 12

Annie opened one eye on Friday morning a few minutes before the alarm was set to go off. Smokey sat next to her bed staring at her, willing her to wake up and dump some food into his bowl. Roxy lifted her head and her tail thumped on the bed.

"Okay. I get the message. You two are ready for the day to begin and I have to get to the café."

The morning routine went like every other morning and Annie and Roxy left the cozy apartment to drive to the café. Annie gave herself a minute to be jealous of Jason's dark house and the luxury of sleeping in.

Wind whipped the trees around as clouds streamed across the early morning light. "If we're lucky, this will be a fast moving storm and the sun will be shining this afternoon for the concert, barbeque and bonfire," she said to Roxy.

After she parked and they were walking to the café, Roxy chased down a blowing leaf. "Right. You take it how it comes don't you?"

Leona's favorite oldie station was blasting when Annie walked into the Cove's Corner building. A mixture of cinnamon, sugar and chocolate aromas drifted in the hallway, getting stronger and stronger as Annie reached the Black Cat Café door.

Danny was busy restocking the books on the freebrary shelves while Leona hummed along to Bruce Springsteen's Fourth of July song.

This is interesting, Annie thought to herself. Danny has never been here so early.

As the door clicked behind Annie, Danny turned toward her and a deep shade of blush traveled up his cheeks.

"Hi Annie. I'm helping Leona this morning."

Annie peeked at Leona and noticed a relaxed smile on her face.

"We drove in together, right Danny?" Leona said, throwing him a kiss.

"Okay, then. Should I leave and come back later?" Annie asked, only half serious.

Leona popped the hot blueberry muffins out of the muffin tin onto cooling racks. "Of course not. It's all your fault we had such a great time last night."

Annie held her hands up. "Too much information." She tied an apron around her waist and got out ingredients to prepare for the lunch sandwiches.

Danny walked to the counter, carefully holding a book in his big hands. "You should take a look at this, Annie."

Annie's hands trembled as she opened the cover of the book and saw another message in red ink. *Annie, you need to do some real digging.*

She read it a second time, out loud for Leona and Danny to hear. "This is the third message I've gotten. I think they're connected to Robbie's death, but I don't know how."

"Did I miss something?" Leona asked. "What were the other messages?"

Annie told them and they both stared with blank expressions.

"At least I can take this book to Tyler and he can check for prints. I lost the other two books when my bag was taken yesterday."

The timer went off, making Leona hustle to the oven to take out several blackberry pies.

Annie poured herself a cup of coffee and sat down at the counter with a bowl of granola. Danny took the stool next to her and Leona put a plate with a big blueberry muffin in front of him before he even had a chance to ask for it.

"Jason keeps telling me to let Tyler handle this but someone is pulling me into the investigation whether I want to be involved or not."

"Where did that book come from, Danny?" Leona asked.

"It was on a table outside on the deck. Someone must have left it there last night."

Mia and Martha came in together but stopped short when Annie turned toward them and they saw the expression on her face.

"Everything all right?" Mia asked, trying not to let her concern come through in her question.

Leona said, "Someone has been leaving Annie messages inside books. She thinks they might be connected to Robbie's death. The third one showed up here this morning."

Mia and Martha looked at the message and Martha offered an idea. "Maybe it has to do with digging up information about Hazel's daughter."

"How do you know about her?" Annie asked, her voice barely audible.

"Everyone *knows* even though no one talked about her. Hazel and Peter had a fling about twenty years ago."

"Jillian looks to be about twenty," Annie said, more to herself than to the others.

"Who's Jillian?" Leona demanded with her hands on her hips. "How come you all know so much more than I do?"

Mia patted Leona's arm. "You haven't been yourself lately." She smiled at Danny.

Danny blushed again as he looked at Leona. He clearly wasn't sure if everyone would approve of him dating Leona.

Leona repeated her question about Jillian.

"Jillian is Hazel's daughter. I met her yesterday and Hazel told me that Robbie wouldn't let Jillian come to the house to visit."

Heads nodded in understanding. Martha whistled. "That certainly adds an interesting twist to Robbie's death." She unfolded a paper. "Have you seen this article that my granddaughter wrote for the Catfish Cove Chronicle?"

Leona took the paper first and scanned the article. "It's official. Robbie's death has been ruled an overdose of insulin. It's being investigated as a homicide." She turned to Annie. "Tell Mia and Martha about the first two messages."

Annie repeated them. "The first one said, *Annie, Oliver knows what happened* and the second one said, *Annie, check the trash*."

Leona looked at the others. "Do any of you know who Oliver is?"

Three heads shook no.

Bob and Harry Crowley entered the café making Martha fluff up her hair and flutter her eyes. Annie hid her laugh behind a fake cough as she took her spot behind the pastry case. Martha had been playing one Crowley twin off the other ever since the Valentine's Day dance. And she loved the attention.

"I think it was that nurse," Bob Crowley said as he stood in front of the pastries.

"No, it couldn't be her, too obvious. What about the real estate developer? He's too slick for my taste," Harry argued.

"Probably was Hazel herself. I don't know how she put up with Robbie for so many years as it is. He always bossed her around like she was useless. And, I wouldn't blame her if she did it," the first twin said.

"Are you two going to argue all morning or put an order in? You're holding up the works here," Martha told Bob and Harry. "And while you're at it, get me a piece of Leona's special blackberry pie. I'll be sitting outside." She winked at Annie and Annie gave her the thumbs up sign.

"What are you laughing at?" Bob asked Annie. "I hope you don't treat your man like Martha treats us." He studied the choices before deciding on two slices of pie. He added a big dollop of whipped cream to both pieces when he poured his coffee.

Harry ordered the same and carried two coffees outside, black for himself and Irish crème for Martha.

"Martha has her hands full with those two," Annie said to Mia after the trio was out of earshot.

"I think you have that backwards. They have their hands full with her! She loves the attention."

Annie noticed Jason standing off to one side with a grin on his face. As soon as everyone was away from the pastry case, he whispered to her, "I like the advice you got from one of the Crowley twins."

"Yeah? How do you know he was referring to you?" Annie teased.

"Ouch. That hurt." He pointed to a cinnamon roll. "I'll have that one please. Any more messages this morning?"

"As a matter of fact, Danny found a book on one of the tables with a new message." She handed him his cinnamon roll.

"Can you sit outside with me?"

"As soon as Bree, Ashley and Kristen get here, I'll take a short break. Save me a seat."

Annie kept her eyes on Jason as he walked through the French doors to the tables on the deck. His limp, which she hadn't noticed in a while, was obvious. Maybe it was the weather. She made a mental note to ask him about it.

A steady stream of customers mobbed the café, keeping Annie's mind busy with easy chit chat about the weather and the upcoming Fourth of July events. It promised to be one of the biggest crowds ever in Catfish Cove.

Annie made sure Bree was all set before she took a quick break to join Jason on the deck. She frowned when she saw Luke Carbone. What was he doing sitting with Jason?

Annie pulled a chair as close to Jason as possible before sitting down.

"Annie, you've already met Luke?"

"Yes. We've met." She glared at Luke, hoping he would get the message he was not welcome at the table, much less at the café.

Luke smiled warmly. "I think we got off on the wrong foot yesterday at the Benson's home. My apologies."

Annie relaxed slightly, but she knew his type: slick and charismatic when they wanted something.

"Hazel told me you were with Robbie the morning before he died. That puts you at the scene of a murder," Annie said.

Jason knocked his knee against Annie's thigh but she kept her eyes glued to Luke's face. A muscle on Luke's cheek twitched even as he tried to put on his most charming smile.

"Hazel heard Robbie arguing. What happened?"

Luke rose from the table abruptly. "I didn't kill that double crossing nasty excuse of a man, but he got just what he deserved. We had a deal and I plan on getting that land." He smiled a forced smile at Annie and added, "Maybe you should be talking to the berry farmer neighbor who went in the house after I left." Luke stomped away without another word.

"What were you doing sitting with that guy, Jason?" Annie demanded after Luke left.

"He contacted me to help him find suitable land for a condo development. That's what I do, find things for people, remember?"

Annie was stunned into silence. "You brought that slick man to Catfish Cove?"

"Hey. Robbie Benson wanted to sell his land. I only pointed them toward each other."

Annie stood up. "Catfish Cove doesn't need condos. We need to protect our open spaces. I can't believe you could think this was a good idea."

Chapter 13

"Uh oh, looks like trouble in paradise," Leona said to Annie, who walked back into the café with a look that could kill.

Annie glared and said nothing. The lunch orders were coming in fast and furious so Annie stayed busy making sandwiches and dishing out chicken salad.

Leona kept the grill sizzling. "What happened? You went outside with a smile on your face and returned with the biggest frown I've ever seen."

"I don't want to talk about it," Annie said between clenched teeth.

Leona whispered in Annie's ear, "You're probably overreacting. Shake it off."

Annie glared.

Mia cleaned vacated tables so arriving customers could find a place to sit and enjoy their food. Ashley and her friend Kristen manned the ice cream window with minimal flirting with the customers, while Bree shot angry glares their way when she thought Leona wouldn't notice.

"Will you help me find a book?" Annie heard a gray haired woman ask Danny who hung around the café all day keeping an eye on the freebrary.

All in all, the café ran like a well-oiled machine. Even with the undercurrents of drama simmering just below the surface.

Until it didn't.

All it took was one obnoxious, hot and hungry tourist, impatient for a table. "I was here first!" His outburst stunned everyone into silence until Jason appeared and led the culprit outside. Annie allowed her own simmering anger toward Jason to cool a bit after watching Jason's performance. She caught his eye and smiled. He winked in reply.

"Everything back on track?" Leona elbowed Annie as she carried a plate to a waiting customer.

"Maybe. I can't let him off the hook too quickly though," Annie said with a grin.

Mia flopped onto a counter stool. "What's the plan for the rest of the afternoon?"

Leona leaned both elbows on the counter. "I'm closing the door in about twenty minutes. Danny's helping me move the portable ice cream freezer to the town green and we'll continue selling ice cream at the chicken barbeque. People can still bring their food over here and sit on the deck if they want, but we won't be serving anything from the café."

Annie whispered, "So? You and Danny?" She raised her eyebrows in question.

Leona glanced left and right. No one was nearby. "Thanks for opening my eyes yesterday. You know how he's such a sweet guy?"

Annie nodded.

"He's sweet and gentle with everything. If you know what I mean." Leona winked.

"I don't need that image, thank you very much. How about his drinking problem?"

"He's got that under control. For now. But I promised to help with that. Seltzer for both of us."

Both Mia and Annie choked on that comment.

Danny awkwardly approached the three giggling women. "Annie, I found this." He handed her a book.

Panic clutched her chest. "Another one? Where did you find it?" Annie asked before she even looked inside.

"On the seat at the table by the window. It was stuck between the seat and the wall."

Annie opened the front cover. Red lettering stared at her. *Annie, it's not what it seems.*

"I'm heading to the police station to show these two books to Tyler. None of the messages make any sense to me."

The messages went round and round in Annie's head as she drove to the police station. They had to be connected to Robbie's death, but how? She hoped with Tyler's help they could figure something out.

The police station was crowded. The officer on duty at the desk told her to take a seat and Tyler would be out as soon as possible. She sighed and found an empty chair in the corner.

"Did you hear there was a murder in town?" a fiftyish year old woman asked the man sitting next to her. "I heard it was a land dispute."

Annie sagged in her chair. Even the tourists were gossiping about Catfish Cove. That couldn't be good.

The man added his two cents. "Maybe it was about love. The only time I was ever mad enough to want someone dead was when my best friend stole my girl." He laughed. "That was a long time ago, and I won you back so good thing I didn't kill that bloke or I would have ended up in jail instead of spending my life with you."

The woman squeezed his hand. "You never told me that before."

Annie's hand went to her heart and she felt slightly guilty for eavesdropping on such a tender moment.

Finally, Tyler walked into the front room and Annie saw him searching for her. She stood up and followed him down the hallway to his office.

"What's going on here today?"

"All the tourists. It happens every year. Parking tickets and silly things like that." He leaned back in his chair. "I have a feeling you're here about something more important than all that stuff."

Annie pulled the two books from her bag and placed them in front of Tyler on his desk.

"I thought you lost the books?"

"I did. These are two new ones. Take a look and see if the messages make any sense to you."

Tyler studied the words, then handed a pen and paper to Annie. "Write down all the messages. One under the other."

She did as he asked.

Annie, Oliver knows what happened
Annie, check the trash
Annie, you need to do some real digging
Annie, it's not what it seems

Tyler took the paper and circled Oliver, trash, digging and not what it seems. "Have you figured out who Oliver is yet?"

Annie shook her head. "Not a clue, and no one else can think of an Oliver either."

"The next clue is the trash." Tyler set a clear bag on his desk. "This is what we took from Robbie's house. Not much in the way of trash."

Annie straightened up and picked up the bag. "Maybe it's what's *not* in the trash. If he died from an overdose, where's the vial?"

"Why didn't I think of that?" Tyler exclaimed.

"Someone took the evidence so the clue wasn't in the trash. Who might have taken the vial?"

Tyler took out his notebook. "Peter Hayworth told me he went to talk to Robbie, and when he left Luke Carbone was driving in. Stacey Jordon says he died before the ambulance arrived. She's the one who called the police. And, of course, Hazel was around. She told me she went out for a walk, so she doesn't have an alibi."

"Wait a minute. Peter told you Luke arrived when he left?"

Tyler checked his notes again. "Yeah."

"Luke Carbone told me he saw Peter going into the house when he was driving out. Someone is lying."

"And, of course, you found Peter unconscious near his blackberry bushes. Was he on his way home from Robbie's house?"

"Good question. He told me he was spreading some new fertilizer and the fumes knocked him out." Annie stood up. "I've got to run. Are you going to the barbeque and bonfire tonight with JC?"

"I'll be there but I'm on duty. JC doesn't have to work so she'll be there with Dylan."

"Everything's going well between you two?" Annie asked.

Tyler nodded and smiled. "She finally can see that you and I are friends and the past is the past. Thanks for letting her know that."

"You two are good together. And it's great to have you as a friend. Maybe it's better this way."

"Maybe. We'll never know, will we?" he said, his eyes downcast.

"See you tonight at the barbeque. I have to check on a dog." Annie left his office before he had a chance to ask any questions. She conveniently left out the part about the dog being at Hazel Benson's house.

Annie and Roxy headed to Hazel's house. She was curious to find out how Zoe was adjusting. Hazel certainly had no trouble making her decision at the animal shelter. She knew exactly what she was looking for.

When Annie knocked on Hazel's door, she heard Zoe bark but no one came to let her in. Annie tried the doorknob and the door opened so she peeked inside and called out Hazel's name. Zoe ran to the door, wagging her tail when she recognized Annie and Roxy.

"Hey Zoe. Where's Hazel?" Annie cocked her head, hoping to hear the sound of footsteps approaching.

Nothing.

Silence.

Annie hesitated but then remembered her promise to Karen at the shelter and made a quick decision to take Zoe for a walk. "Hazel must be around somewhere," she said to the dogs, feeling annoyed. "If she doesn't turn up, I'll have to take Zoe home with me."

Zoe happily flew out the door chasing Roxy around the yard. Annie walked around the side of the house where she could see Peter's blackberry fields in the distance.

"Come on girls, let's go this way." Annie wasn't sure what she had in mind but something pulled her toward the rows of berry bushes.

She found the shovel still stuck in the ground where she found Peter on Wednesday. She sniffed the air and noticed just a faint bit of the awful smell lingering. She checked her watch and calculated the time it took to walk between Hazel's house and the spot where she found Peter unconscious. Only ten minutes. Annie pulled out the shovel and stabbed it into a different spot. The shovel hit something, a rock probably.

"What are you doing?" a deep voice asked.

Chapter 14

"Peter. You startled me. I'm taking Roxy and Hazel's new dog, Zoe, for a walk. They ran in this direction."

Both dogs bounded back, sniffing Peter and begging for attention or a treat, or possibly hoping for both. He reached in his pocket and pulled out a couple of treats. "I like to be prepared," he said to Annie as he offered one to each dog. "Why are you taking Hazel's dog for a walk? Shouldn't she be doing that?" Peter asked as he pulled out the shovel and tamped the soil back into place.

"I promised Karen at the shelter to help with Zoe since this is Hazel's first dog, and I didn't see Hazel when I stopped at the house." Annie patted both dogs, one on each side of her.

"I've been looking for this shovel. It must have been here ever since I passed out."

They both turned when a panicked voice called Zoe several times.

"I better get her back to Hazel, she sounds worried." Annie started to walk away but turned back to Peter. "Are you going to the barbeque and bonfire later?"

"Definitely. It's what Kirk, Emily and the grandkids came for. My drama at the ER was just an added bonus." He chuckled. "Well, and the fireworks tomorrow night."

Annie waved and jogged after the disappearing dogs. At least they were headed in the right direction.

By the time Annie got to the house, Hazel was crouched down with Zoe jumping up and licking her face. "How did you get out of the house?"

"It's my fault. Sorry. I called you but you didn't answer."

Hazel stood up, unsmiling. "You walked into my house?"

"No, I didn't go in, I only called through a crack in the door and Zoe was excited to see me. Were you inside?"

"I'm not sure it's any of your business what I was doing. Come on Zoe." Hazel disappeared into the house with Zoe and without another word to Annie.

A black Lexus sedan sped up the driveway and stopped behind Annie's Subaru. Luke Carbone emerged in his fitted suit and spit-shined shoes which got covered in dust as soon as his foot hit the ground. Roxy ran over to greet him but Luke was in no mood for conversing with a dog.

"Where's Hazel? I left her a message that I was stopping by."

Annie snapped her fingers to get Roxy away from Luke. "I'm not her keeper, but I have the distinct impression that she isn't one bit interested in selling off her land. Especially to you. For condos."

"Well, she can at least listen to the offer I'm prepared to make, and with her brother out of the way, it will be a nice piece of change in her pocket. Otherwise, without a job, she'll lose the land and I'll get it at foreclosure price."

"Who told you she doesn't have a job?" Annie tried to keep from laughing.

"Robbie. He told me he's been taking care of her for her whole life and he promised he'd get her to sign the papers." Luke moved closer to Annie. "I suspect it's going to be a lot easier and cheaper to deal with Hazel now."

"That sounds like quite the motive to get Robbie out of the picture," Annie said as she crossed her arms and smirked at Luke.

Luke's face turned red with anger as he leaned right into Annie's face. "I already told you, he was very much alive when I left."

"If you say so." She enjoyed baiting him.

The front door opened. "Leave her alone. I'll talk to you, but Annie comes in too."

Annie's blood started to boil. First Hazel ignored her and now expected her to help. Something was wrong with the picture as far as Annie was concerned.

"I don't have time now." She checked her watch. "The chicken barbeque is starting and I'm supposed to be there to help." Annie smiled. "How about you both come too?" She crossed her fingers inside her pocket. At least, she'd be able to keep an eye on them.

Hazel hesitated. "Okay. Can I bring Zoe?"

"As long as she's on a leash." Annie gave herself a mental head slap. Why did she let herself get dragged into the middle of this battle?

Roxy and Zoe sat in the back seat, panting with excitement and hanging their heads out the window. Annie checked her rearview mirror and saw Luke's car following behind.

"What are you going to say to Luke about the land? He's convinced you need the money and will sell."

Hazel smiled. "That's good to know. I'm planning to string him along and keep him in town until Robbie's murder is solved."

"Very clever. You're convinced it's murder and not an accidental overdose?"

"I never thought it could be an accidental overdose. My instinct tells me this will play out even better than the murders in my stories. I have to find out how it ends so I can work it into the book I'm writing now."

Annie felt the hairs on her arm prickle. What had Stacey told her? Hazel's stories always implicated the wrong person. Was that her plan? Point the evidence in a real murder toward an innocent person for an idea for one of her stories?

The town green was mobbed with people. Annie had to drive way down Main Street before she could find a spot to park. Luke swerved into the space in front of her and hustled to catch up with them.

"How about I treat you ladies to a chicken dinner?" Luke offered in his best salesman voice.

Much to Annie's surprise, Hazel accepted the offer. Annie declined, saying she had to work.

Annie followed behind Hazel and Luke, listening to his sales pitch for the condo development and how wealthy the land deal would make Hazel. She nodded, and from all outward appearances, seemed to be taking it all in.

The town green was covered with stalls selling everything from food to hand-made crafts plus games and face-painting for the kids. Annie wove her way through the crowd.

The ice cream booth that Leona set up had a long line of people, mostly kids, waiting to be served. Leona and Mia had their hands full scooping ice cream so Annie tied an apron on and pitched in.

"It's about time you showed up," Leona said in a not too friendly tone.

Annie ignored the comment and helped the next person in line. "I bet I can guess what you want," Annie said to her friend JC's son.

"Mint chocolate chip with hot fudge sauce," Dylan said with a big grin on his face.

"With sprinkles on top too, right?"

"Yes."

"How about you JC?"

JC was searching the crowd. "What?"

"Any ice cream for you?" Annie repeated.

"No thanks. I'm trying to find Tyler. He's working, but if there's no trouble he's supposed to meet us here." Suddenly, she jumped up and waved. "There he is."

Annie handed the cup to Dylan and scooped ice cream into a cone. When Tyler joined JC, Annie handed him the cone. "You look like you could use something cold. Here's your favorite, blackberry ice cream in a sugar cone. No charge."

When Tyler thanked Annie, she noticed a slight frown on JC's face. Or was she imagining it? Maybe JC was still jealous about the fact that Tyler and Annie had been engaged a few years back.

Mia elbowed Annie. "I'm going to get some chicken, do you want one too? It's Bob and Harry Crowley's specialty. They only do it once a year on the third of July."

"Of course."

"They roped Martha into helping them this year. She made aprons for the twins to wear."

"Oh yeah? I'll have to check that out when I get a chance."

Mia laughed. "Martha found material covered with roosters cock-a-doodle-doing. She said it matched Bob and Harry's personality. She told her granddaughter to make sure and get a photo for the front page of the paper."

Leona pushed her way into the conversation. "What's that slimy Luke Carbone doing here? I'd hoped he'd be out of town by now."

"The best I can figure out, Hazel is keeping him around for a story idea," Annie explained.

A crease formed between Leona's eyes. "What kind of story?"

"She writes murder mysteries. She told me she needs to find out how Robbie's murder plays out so she can use the idea in the book she's writing."

"Seriously? What is wrong with her?"

Annie shrugged.

The band set up in the gazebo and started their concert. Annie relaxed into the background rhythm and reminded herself how lucky she was to be living in Catfish Cove with this holiday tradition of food, music and spectacular fireworks. Even with the extra drama of Robbie's death, she loved Catfish Cove, especially in the summer.

"Hey. Can I get some ice cream over here?"

Annie swiveled her head to see a smiling Jason. She forced the corners of her mouth to stop twitching into a smile. "I'm still mad at you."

"About that. I'm happy to spend all the time it takes to apologize." He gave her his best sorry puppy dog eyes which made her lips twitch even more.

Annie held an apron out to Jason. "Help me in here, and when Mia gets back I'll let you try to change my mind." Her mouth finally won and she rewarded him with a smile.

Annie watched Jason scoop ice cream and talk to the customers. He had such an easy way about him it was impossible to stay angry.

A panicked voice interrupted Annie's thoughts. "Zoe's missing."

Chapter 15

Hazel fidgeted as if she couldn't figure out what to do with her body parts. "I made a mistake coming here. Zoe disappeared into thin air."

Annie patted her arm. "Tell me exactly what happened. Maybe she wandered off with another dog."

"Luke kept chattering my ear off about his ridiculous condo plans, and when he handed me some papers to read, I must have let go of Zoe's leash."

"Can you remember anyone hanging around where you were sitting?"

Hazel closed her eyes and stood perfectly still. "A teenage boy had been crouching down petting Zoe. He had dark, longish hair, a black t-shirt." Hazel's eyes opened but Annie decided she was still recalling the scene. "He had a nose ring. Gold." She rubbed her own nose.

Jason silently nodded, indicating that he would stay at the ice cream booth. Annie's fingers tightened on Hazel's arm. "Come on."

She walked through the crowd to the north side of the green which was the high point and gave a better view of all the activity. Scanning heads, nothing unusual jumped to her attention and she admitted that it would be hard to see Zoe. "Let's circle around the outside."

The head of a dark haired boy caught Annie's attention. He lounged against a tree. As Annie moved closer, she recognized him as the boy that Bree ran off with and Zoe lay on the ground by his feet, happily chewing on something.

"Stay here," she told Hazel.

Annie and Roxy approached the boy. "Nice dog." Zoe leaped up at the familiar voice, jumping on Annie and Roxy. "Where'd she come from?" Annie asked the nervous teenager.

The boy shifted from one foot to the other, obviously not prepared for the question. "What's it to you?" he mumbled.

Annie pointed to Tyler who was standing about twenty feet away talking to a group of people. "See that police officer over there?"

The boy nodded.

"He's a very good friend of mine. As a matter of fact, we were engaged at one time." She paused to let the impact of that information sink in. "How about I ask him to come over and chat with you about this dog?"

"Some guy said it was a practical joke," he blurted out.

"What guy?"

"I don't know. He was dressed kind of fancy and he gave me twenty dollars to take the dog and give her a marrow bone. I wasn't going to keep her. Here." He pulled a twenty dollar bill from his pocket and stuffed it into Annie's hand along with Zoe's leash. "Apologize to the lady for me."

He tried to hurry away but Annie grabbed his arm. "Apologize yourself." She wasn't going to let this punk get away that easily. Maybe if he had to look Hazel in the eye, he'd understand the full weight of what he had done.

Annie pulled him to Hazel. The boy kicked his toe in the grass. Annie elbowed him in the side.

"Sorry," he mumbled.

"Sorry for what?" Annie demanded.

Finally, he looked at Hazel. "Sorry for taking your dog. I didn't mean any harm."

Annie released his arm and he disappeared like a puff of smoke. "Someone dressed in fancy clothes paid him twenty dollars to take Zoe." Annie handed the twenty to Hazel.

They both looked toward the bench where Hazel had been sitting with Luke Carbone. He was nowhere in sight.

"Do you think it was Luke?" Hazel whispered.

"I don't know for sure, but that would be my guess."

As Annie kept her eyes on Hazel, she saw her mouth turn down into a frown. Following Hazel's focus, Annie saw Jillian laughing with Peter Hayworth.

They both had the same odd crooked smile.

"Does she know?" Annie asked Hazel.

Hazel quickly turned back toward Annie. "What are you talking about?"

Annie moved her eyes from Hazel to Jillian. "Jillian and Peter."

"Is it that obvious?"

Yes, she thought, but replied, "Probably not to everyone." Most people weren't searching for clues to Robbie's death.

"Once Robbie figured out Peter was Jillian's father, he wanted revenge. He hated Peter. I think that was his motivation to sell the land."

Annie steered Hazel back to the edge of the green, a quieter place to talk. "Robbie still needed you to sign the papers."

"He was certain I would agree so I could have Jillian back in my life." Her shoulders sagged.

Jillian put her arm around Hazel's shoulders. "Mom, I'm surprised to see you here. You never come to these events."

"I'm turning over a new leaf." They walked off, arm in arm, with Zoe happily trotting next to Hazel.

Annie felt the presence of someone next to her.

"I saw you watching us. You figured it out, didn't you?"

"I did. When did Robbie figure it out?" Annie asked Peter.

Peter chewed on his lower lip. "I'm not sure. My guess is right around when he started looking for a buyer for his land. I had made him offers over the years and he knew I was dead set against having that good farmland developed. And condos? That made my blood boil."

There was a lot of anger hidden beneath Peter's easy going manner, Annie realized. Enough to make him a killer? Probably, if the opportunity was presented.

"I didn't kill Robbie," Peter said, as if he had read Annie's thoughts.

Maybe yes, maybe no. He was in the house that day. "What do you think Hazel will do with the land now?"

His eyes softened. "She'll keep it for Jillian."

"You would like having Jillian living next door." Annie didn't ask this as a question, but made a logical statement. "No condos and your daughter nearby, a win-win for you."

Peter cleared his throat. "I know what you're thinking, Annie, and I don't like it. Why don't you let the police do the investigating before you discover something you don't want to know?"

"Are you threatening me, Peter?"

He stared at her for several long seconds before walking away.

Peter's true colors were revealed when he had to deal with a conflict. Annie filed those comments away.

"Hey, what happened to Hazel and Zoe?" Jason rested his arm on Annie's shoulder.

"Jillian found them."

Jason turned Annie to face him. "Something's on your mind. Spit it out."

Bits and pieces of conversation floated through her mind but nothing fit together into a neat, tidy package. Yet. She smiled at Jason. "I'm starving. Is there delicious barbequed chicken waiting for me?"

"Sorry, I ate it." He took her hand. "I'll get you some hot chicken, fresh off the grill."

Jason and Annie waited in line for Bob and Harry Crowley's world famous barbequed chicken. Maybe not world famous, but Catfish Cove famous at least. With their colorful aprons on and Martha bossing them around, the trio made an entertaining show.

"Those chicken legs are burning!" Martha scolded.

"No they aren't. We've been doing this for fifty years. Watch out," one of the twins cautioned as he stepped around Martha.

Martha put her hands on her ample hips. "Do you want my help or not?"

"Not really," they both chimed in at the same time.

Martha stared with her mouth hanging open. She tore off her apron and stomped away from the grill. "I never," she muttered under her breath.

Annie nudged Jason and they both giggled behind their hands. "She had steam coming out of her ears. Those twins will regret treating Martha like that."

"Two grilled chickens please," Jason said to Harry Crowley who stared in disbelief at Martha's retreating figure.

"What just happened?" he said, mostly to himself, while he handed two plates to Jason.

"Maybe you should go and apologize," Jason suggested.

As if that thought never occurred to Harry, he turned his gaze to Jason and nodded. Without a word to his brother, he dashed after Martha.

"She's going to tell him a thing or two," Annie said as she and Jason walked away from the grilling area. "Let's find a spot to sit and eat this delicious chicken before they light the bonfire."

The green overlooked Heron Lake and every year on the third of July, the fire department constructed a huge bonfire in the sand at the edge of the lake. Kids of all ages danced around with red, white and blue paraphernalia, star shaped glasses, sparklers, and outrageous costumes.

Jason spread a blanket away from the biggest crowds and they settled down comfortably together.

"What's the secret ingredient in the chicken marinade?" Annie asked between bites. "Maybe Martha can bribe it out of Harry in exchange for getting back in his good graces."

They finished the chicken, down to every finger licking drip, seconds before the bonfire lit up the sky. Oohs and ahhs filled the air.

Annie scanned the crowd, enjoying all the happiness until her eyes settled on two figures exposed by the bonfire. Luke and Peter's son, Kirk, stood in what had been the shadows, seriously discussing something and completely ignoring the excitement all around them.

Chapter 16

The sun promised to be bright and hot when it peaked over the mountain early Saturday morning. Annie stretched under her cool cotton sheet and smiled at the memory of Jason's company the previous night.

Until she heard a soft thunk in her living room.

Roxy growled and rushed into the other room. Annie's heart raced, but not with fear this time. It was more from a shot of adrenalin mixed with anger that some cowardly person kept sending her anonymous messages inside of books.

Picking the book off the floor, she was shocked to see it was a book written by Summer Spring. Inside, the message said, *Annie, you're getting closer. Don't give up.*

Was it Hazel sending her these messages? Or did someone want her to think it was Hazel?

"Come on Roxy, we need a walk."

Slipping quickly into comfy shorts, t-shirt and flip-flops, Annie grabbed her camera and quietly left her apartment with Roxy. At this early hour, she hoped she would have the Lake Trail to herself. Roxy ran ahead, sniffing the scents from all the overnight visitors.

Annie walked with a purpose, stopping occasionally to take photos. Having her camera in front of her eye helped her tune out the rest of the world so she missed the sound of jogging footsteps coming closer until a voice spooked her.

"You're an early bird."

Annie felt her hands tighten on her camera. "Yes, in the hopes of having the trail to myself," she answered brusquely.

Luke put his hand on her shoulder and she tensed. Was he the one to slip the book through her cat door as he jogged by her apartment? Hazel had a stack of books in her kitchen, anyone could have taken one.

"Hazel seems to like you. Can you help me talk some sense into her?"

Annie finally lowered her camera and turned to face him. "Why would I do that?"

"Well, for one, she'd make a ton of money and condos would be good for Catfish Cove. More people would mean more money flowing into local businesses. I like it here and would like to make it my home."

Annie smiled but inside she told herself Luke was the last person she wanted to move to Catfish Cove. His fancy car and fancy shoes didn't fit in at all. Although, she did admit to herself, he looked casually decent in his jogging clothes. She shook that thought from her head.

"Tell me, Luke, what did you and Robbie Benson discuss the morning before he was murdered?" Yes, she said murdered, hoping it would shock Luke enough to tell her something useful.

His jaw clenched. "Fair enough. I'm asking for your help so I'll answer your question. I got to his house mid to late morning. He had promised to sign the papers to sell me his land, but when I found him in his living room, he was acting odd."

"Odd?"

"He didn't make much sense when he talked to me, like he was confused. I was angry and left."

"Did you see Hazel?"

"No. She always avoided me. I depended completely on Robbie to get her to sign the papers."

"Did you see anyone?"

Luke gazed out over the lake. "It's beautiful here. Were you up early enough to see the sunrise?"

Annie nodded, keeping quiet to give him time to tell the rest of the story. She knew he had more to share if he wanted to, even though she wasn't positive she believed his version of events.

"I did see someone else. Two someones, as a matter of fact."

Annie felt herself flinch. She hadn't seen that coming.

"When I drove out, I checked my rear view mirror and Peter Hayworth was lurking by the side of the house with a young woman. She looked to be twentyish, attractive, with a long braid over one shoulder."

"Jillian," Annie blurted out before she could stop herself. "Are you positive?"

"Yes. Peter headed toward the house but the woman stayed by the side of the house. Who's Jillian?"

"Hazel's daughter." Annie touched Luke's arm. "Thank you for the information. I have to get to work."

"Wait. Will you help me?"

"I'll let you know. I have some things to figure out first."

By the time Annie and Roxy were back in front of Cobblestone Cottage, mouthwatering aromas seeped from Jason's window and she bolted through his door.

"That's a graceful entrance." Jason grinned as Annie leaned on his counter to catch her breath.

"I had an interesting chat with Luke Carbone."

Jason raised one eyebrow as he folded his omelet. "How about I share my delicious pepper and cheese omelet with you while you fill me in on your conversation with the enemy."

He took another plate from the cupboard, sliced his spatula through the omelet and slid half on a plate for Annie and half for himself, handing her both plates to carry to the table. Jason brought toast, coffee and orange juice.

"Okay. Eat first?" He laughed when he realized Annie's fork was already in her mouth.

After she wolfed down about half of the food, Annie set her fork on the plate. "I found another book with a message on my floor this morning."

"Never a dull moment in your life, is there? Are you going to keep me in suspense, or share the words of wisdom?"

"This one said, *Annie, you're getting closer, don't give up*." Her shoulders did a little forward roll.

"Closer to what? I get the feeling all the messages are just a wild goose chase. And—"

"There's more?" Jason interrupted.

"And, the message was written in a book by Summer Spring."

"Who? What kind of name is that?"

"It's Hazel's penname."

Jason put his fork down. "Do you think Hazel left you all these messages?"

"Maybe. Maybe not."

He chuckled. "You're right, it has to be one or the other. What about your chat with Luke Carbone, your favorite tourist in Catfish Cove? Did he share anything of significance with you?" Jason's eyes twinkled with amusement.

"Luke said Robbie was confused and talking nonsense when he was at the house on Wednesday morning. And," she paused, "he saw two people lurking by the side of the house when he drove out."

Jason leaned forward. "That's something. Another suspect?"

"It was Jillian with Peter."

Jason rested his chin on his left hand and let that information sink in. "What does it all mean?"

Annie gobbled down the rest of her omelet, then pushed herself up from the table. "I don't know, but someone knows what happened and I think Hazel knows more than she has told me."

"Where are you going?"

"To the café. Leona's going to eat me alive for being so late. I'm only working through the morning because Roxy and I are in the pet parade at noon along with Karen and a bunch of the shelter dogs. Want to help us?" Annie leveled her best pleading eyes on Jason until he had to laugh at her pathetic attempt to make him feel guilty.

"Of course I'll help. Do you want me to dress up in my best Fourth of July attire too?"

Annie clapped her hands. "I was hoping you'd say that. See you at the café, no later than noon. The parade starts in the parking lot."

Jason mumbled something under his breath that sounded a lot like, "Why didn't I lock my door this morning?"

Annie made it to the café mere minutes before opening time. Leona glared, Mia sighed with relief and Danny said, "Good morning Annie."

What a nice guy. You could always count on Danny to be in the moment with a warm smile. Annie hoped Leona didn't break his fragile heart.

The door opened, bringing in a steady stream of customers. Blackberry pies, cinnamon rolls and blueberry muffins flew out of the pastry case. The faces moved through in a blur of friendly chatter until one voice attracted Annie's attention.

"Maybe you can talk some sense into my father."

Annie looked into Kirk Hayworth's face, and it wasn't a friendly expression she was met with. "Excuse me?"

"My father. He's decided to hire his odd neighbor's daughter to help him on the farm. Why her? He's always disliked those people."

"Do you mean Jillian?"

Chapter 17

"Is that her name? She showed up out of thin air and my father is gaga over her."

The customer behind Kirk leaned around him and rudely asked, "Are you going to order or just talk all morning?

"Kirk, I can't talk about this now," Annie said, wanting to move on to the paying customers.

He waved his hand at her dismissively. "Never mind. I hoped you were different."

When there was a lull in customers, Danny sidled over to Annie. "Who was that guy giving you a hard time earlier?"

"Peter Hayworth's son, Kirk. He's upset about decisions his dad is making about the farm. I don't know why he thinks I can help him."

"Well, he left this outside on one of the tables." Danny gave Annie a book.

She opened it to see another message, *Annie, be careful who you talk to.* "Are you sure it was Kirk who left it?"

"Well, I didn't actually see him put it there, but I noticed it after he walked by."

Annie rushed out to the deck, searching for Kirk's face and was relieved to see him sitting at the far side, away from everyone.

She slammed the book on the table in front of him. "Did you leave this for me?"

Kirk looked at Annie with his eyebrows raised in surprise. "I don't know what you're talking about."

Annie settled into a chair next to him and slid the book onto her lap.

"What do you think I can do?" Annie asked Kirk, referring to his earlier request for help.

He rested his arms on the table. "I have no idea. Something is strange about what's happening and my father always talks so highly about you. He never listens to what I have to say."

"I'm flattered, but we have never discussed how he runs his business. You would have more influence about that."

Kirk stared off into space. He drummed his fingers on the table.

Annie leaned forward. "Do you know something else?"

Suddenly, he swiveled toward Annie. "Here's the thing," he said quietly. "I arrived at my father's house Wednesday morning."

Annie nodded. Her stomach flip-flopped, wondering what Kirk knew about the morning Robbie died.

"My dad was fit to be tied. He knew it was the day Robbie was supposed to sign the papers to sell the land to the condo developer. That's why I went to the farm in the morning. I was afraid Dad might do something stupid."

"Do you think he killed Robbie?" Annie asked in disbelief.

Kirk shook his head, his eyes filled with concern. "I don't know. He was ranting and raving and stormed out of the house before I could stop him. I don't know what he did. And now Jillian is working her way into the farm."

"What do you know about Jillian?"

Kirk's head shot up and his eyes narrowed. "What do you mean? I don't know her at all."

Annie's thoughts danced in her head. Jillian was Kirk's half-sister. What would that information do to him? She made up her mind, reaching her hand out to cover Kirk's hand. The touch startled him.

"Thank you for sharing your concerns with me," Annie said. "Here comes Jillian, you could talk to her yourself. Maybe you're making more out of this than you should." Annie stood up as Jillian stopped at the table.

Kirk pushed his chair back. "I have nothing to say to her." He spit the words out to Annie without even glancing at Jillian.

Jillian slumped into Kirk's vacated chair. "I've supremely mucked this up." She looked up at Annie. "Did you tell him?"

"That Peter's your dad?"

Jillian nodded.

"No, the words almost came out of my mouth, but he should hear it from his dad, not me."

Annie hoped she wasn't missed inside as she sat back down with Jillian. "Why were you with Peter outside your mother's house the day Robbie died?"

Jillian's eyes opened wide with surprise.

"He wanted to know if my mother had signed the papers. He said he had already asked Robbie, but Robbie only laughed in his face." She dropped her head. "I was trying to calm him down."

Annie put her hand on Jillian's arm. "What did Peter do after you talked to him?"

She looked away. "I think he went home."

"And what about Luke? Did you see him go in to talk to Robbie?"

"He drove out when I was talking to Peter." She pulled on the hair at the tip of her braid.

Annie considered her answers and wondered if Peter did go back into the house after Luke left. Who was lying to her?

Annie set the book with the message on the table. "Why have you been leaving me messages?"

Jillian's mouth fell open. She whispered, "How did you know it was me?"

"I didn't. Until now." She glared at Jillian. "What are you hiding?"

Karen, from the animal shelter, hollered and waved to Annie, saving Jillian from having to answer a difficult question. "We're getting organized in the parking lot for the pet parade. Are you coming?"

"I'll be right there." Annie stood up and told Jillian, "You have some explaining to do."

Roxy and Annie walked around the building to join the small crowd of people and dogs. Peter's daughter, Emily, was off to one side with her two kids. Logan jumped up and down when he spotted Annie.

"There she is. There's Annie and Roxy," Logan pointed.

Annie waved, happy that Peter gave Emily the message to bring the kids to the pet parade. Logan had an American flag t-shirt on and Ariel had a red, white and blue ballerina outfit. Annie stuck on her headband with star shaped flags sticking up and joined Emily.

She crouched down to Ariel's level. "You have the most beautiful outfit on. Would you like a balloon to carry?"

Ariel nodded enthusiastically, staring at the stars on Annie's headband. "This color." She pointed to the red in her outfit.

"Of course. How about you Logan?" Annie asked.

"Blue, please."

Annie returned with the red and blue balloons.

Karen held both hands up. "Thanks for coming everyone. We have a special person to lead the parade this year."

Annie saw the back of a red, white and blue top hat next to Karen. Her hand covered a laugh when she saw the hat turn around and Jason's grinning face appear. She hadn't expected him to dress up—her comment about a costume was meant to be a teasing joke—but seeing him decked out like Uncle Sam, she had to admit he fit the part quite handsomely.

She put two thumbs up and shook the little star flags sticking above her own head to make them wiggle. She knew they looked pathetic compared to his effort—top hat, red and white vertically striped pants, a blue jacket with tails and red and white striped lapels, and the biggest surprise of all, a white goatee.

Ariel tugged on Annie's hand. "What is it honey?"

"I have to pee."

Annie found Emily busy texting on her cell phone and handed Ariel over to her mom, explaining where to find the bathroom.

"I'll wait here with Logan and Roxy."

All the volunteers in various red, white and blue attire lined up with the shelter dogs, also with patriotic collars or bandanas. Annie handed Roxy's leash to Logan so she had her hands free to take some candid photos. This was an opportunity too colorful to ignore and would be perfect for her Candid Around Catfish Cove photography exhibit.

The lens of her camera zeroed in on an unexpected participant. Hazel stood quietly with Zoe. She even had on a red and white striped shirt and Zoe had a red, white and blue bandana tied around her neck.

Emily returned with Ariel, and Annie made her way with Roxy and the two kids closer to the front of the line to keep an eye on Jason's maneuvers. A red mustang convertible pulled out of the parking lot to start the parade. It was a motley assortment of dogs, many already adopted from the shelter, accompanied by their forever families and about two dozen shelter dogs still hoping to be to find homes.

Tyler had police cars flashing blue lights on the street to stop traffic between the Cove's Corner parking lot and the town green, a half mile at the most. Logan stood tall and proud holding Roxy's leash and Ariel kept one hand on Roxy's back and the other tucked into Annie's hand.

Peter Hayworth drove the convertible with Emily in the passenger seat throwing candy to the kids watching from the sidewalk and Kirk sat in the backseat, unsmiling.

How interesting, Annie thought, everyone who was at the Benson house the day Robbie died showed up for the parade. Except Jillian and Luke Carbone.

Chapter 18

Once everyone arrived on the green, Annie gave Jason the responsibility of watching Roxy and the two kids while she took advantage of the opportunity for more photos. Many would end up with Karen for her bulletin board of successful adoptions and the rest might be part of her opening day photography exhibit.

Emily watched as her kids wandered around with Jason, petting all the dogs. The dogs available for adoption were grouped all together on one side of the green and Annie made sure to take lots of photos. Her camera caught Ariel crouching with her head cocked in front of a small yellow lab mix as if she was in deep conversation with the pup. Much to Ariel's delight, the pup licked her face.

"Mommy. Mommy. Can we keep this one?" Ariel shouted, loud enough for everyone to hear.

Emily talked to the volunteer about the adorable puppy and Annie kept her fingers crossed, hoping for a happy ending.

Jason stood behind Annie, his shadow suddenly engulfing her. He leaned close to her ear. "Uncle Sam thinks you're the most beautiful girl here."

Annie shivered and leaned back to rest against Jason's body. "Uncle Sam caught the attention of all the ladies today. You can have the pick of the lot."

"I like the sound of that. I know which one I'll pick."

"Do tell, Uncle Sam," Annie said, still not turning around.

"If you accompany me to the fireworks tonight, I'll give you a clue."

Annie giggled. "Will Uncle Sam still be wearing this fine outfit?"

She heard a groan. "Uncle Sam needs to return the outfit in," Jason checked his watch, "exactly one half hour or he'll turn into a melted puddle of red, white and blue."

Annie finally turned to face Jason. She saw the sweat dripping down his face. "Oh. I didn't think about how hot it would be. Stand with these dogs waiting to be adopted for one photo, then you can go change."

Jason did as requested and even managed a genuine smile for the camera before hustling to his car.

Emily asked Annie for help deciding about the little mixed breed Ariel fell in love with.

The puppy was given the name Bandit since she had the annoying, but charming, habit of stealing shoes when she was at her foster home. The volunteer was quick to explain that Bandit didn't chew up the shoes, she liked to make a pile on her dog bed. Bandit was great with kids and was good with the basic sit, down, stay commands. And, best of all, she loved everyone.

Annie picked Bandit up and stared into her eyes. "What do you think little girl? Would you want to live with Emily, Ariel and Logan?"

Bandit yipped and wiggled all over.

Annie handed Bandit to Emily. "She says it's the perfect family for her."

Ariel and Logan stood still, holding their breath and holding each other's hands, waiting for their mother to make a decision.

Emily nodded. Both kids jumped up and Bandit yipped again. Annie beamed; another dog she helped find a home. She lifted her camera and captured the two ecstatic children hugging Bandit. Pure, genuine happiness on all three faces.

The volunteer brought Emily to the table set up for signing the adoption papers while Annie kept an eye on Bandit and the kids. Other dogs were also finding homes and the line at the table grew.

Hazel and Zoe joined Annie. "Thank you for helping me find Zoe. I want to help the shelter more if I can."

"Of course. Karen always needs volunteers to walk the dogs. She has a schedule and you let her know when you're available."

"I want to do more than that." Hazel drifted into her own world before continuing. "When I was little, I had a dog and she was my best friend, the one I could always count on, the one I could tell my stories to. Robbie didn't like her and one day she disappeared. I never knew what happened and I was never allowed to have another pet."

Annie stroked Hazel's arm. "That's terrible."

"I'd like to help start a program for therapy dogs. I've read about it." She looked at Annie. "Would you help me?"

"Well, I, ah, don't know anything about a program like that, but I'm sure Karen would be a good resource. We can discuss it with her, but I doubt she has the room or the money for something so ambitious."

Hazel nodded. "That's the part I can help with. I have the land and the money, you and Karen can figure out the rest."

Annie's mouth fell open. "Wow, Hazel. You certainly are filled with surprises." Annie didn't want to discuss it now, but she had a strong suspicion that

Hazel was hiding a few more surprises about the day Robbie died.

"I need to talk to you about Jillian."

Hazel stiffened. "What about her?"

"She's been sending me messages about the day Robbie died but I don't understand them. Can you take a look at them and see if they mean anything to you?"

"Robbie." Hazel spit the word out. "I'm glad he's gone and I don't care who hears me say it. My life has so many new possibilities without his overbearing bullying." She turned her piercing blue eyes on Annie. "Can you understand that?"

Hazel's eyes were so intense, Annie had to look away before Hazel figured out Annie's thoughts. Not that her thoughts came to a nice neat conclusion about what happened to Robbie. Not yet. All the trails from Hazel, Luke, Peter and Jillian weaved in and out and stopped abruptly before leading to any answer.

All Annie managed to utter to Hazel was, "I think I can understand," before they were interrupted by Martha's loud hello.

Hazel moved away with Zoe when Martha barged in, all smiles. "Guess what?" she asked Annie.

"You're here to adopt one of the shelter dogs?"

"Oh. Is that what all these people are doing? No." She whispered in Annie's ear, "Harry proposed to me last night during the bonfire."

That got Annie's attention.

"He left Bob at the grill and apologized about being rude to me and asked me right then and there. Right in the middle of a crowd of people, he got down on one knee and asked me to marry him. Everyone clapped."

"How could you tell it was Harry and not Bob asking you?"

Martha's eyes crinkled at the corners. "I made them aprons and the roosters on Harry's apron were red and the ones on Bob's were yellow. Sneaky, huh?" She laughed so hard she had to cross her legs.

"What did you say?"

Martha held her hand out to show a small diamond engagement ring on her left hand. "I said yes, you ninny. How many proposals will I be getting at my age?"

Annie held Martha's hand to get a good look at the ring. "He had the ring with him?"

"He said it was his plan all along. He's been carrying this ring around in his pocket for weeks, waiting for the right moment. Those were his words. I think he was working up the courage, and when I stalked off he panicked."

Annie hugged Martha. "Congratulations! When's the wedding?"

"As soon as possible. Neither one of us is getting any younger."

The crowd of people began to thin out. Annie started to walk toward the adoption table, but stopped and asked Martha, "How did Bob take it?"

Martha shrugged. "He's not talking to Harry at the moment, but I'm sure they'll work it out. Nothing has ever gotten between their special twin relationship for long."

Until now, Annie thought, but decided to keep those sentiments to herself. Martha might be biting off even more than she could chew.

Karen was organizing all the adoption papers when Annie finally found a chance to talk to her. "How did it go today?"

Karen's smile said it all. "Thanks to your Uncle Sam, we had the biggest turnout ever. Eight dogs adopted today and several people are on the fence but I'm sure some of them will be coming back to the shelter. Once those chocolate puppy dog eyes worm into your heart, it's nearly impossible to walk away for good."

Annie patted Roxy who sat patiently by her side. "Yes, true words for sure. Want to take a look at the photos I took?"

"Of course." Karen walked around the table.

Annie scrolled backwards through her photos and they laughed or oohed and aahed over the best shots. Annie lowered her camera when the dog photos changed to her photos from around Catfish Cove.

"Wait. Can I see the rest?" Karen asked.

"Sure. The rest of the photos I've been taking are for my gallery show, Candid Around Catfish Cove."

They looked at photos of Heron Lake, tourists around town, all the way back to the day Annie walked in Peter Hayworth's fields on Wednesday.

"You're an amazing photographer. Your show will provide a fantastic view of our special town."

Annie moved back to a photograph of Peter's blackberry field and zoomed in. She held the camera for Karen to look at and pointed to a shape. "What do you see here?"

Karen squinted. "It looks like a woman."

"That's what I thought too." Annie picked up her bag and slid her camera strap over her shoulder.

"Where are you going?" Karen asked.

"To see a woman."

Chapter 19

When Annie threw her bag over her shoulder, its weight reminded her about the books with the new messages. If she hurried, she could catch Tyler at the police station before heading to Hazel's house.

JC was busy at the dispatcher desk, so Annie walked down the hall to Tyler's office. Her soft tap on his open door distracted him from his paperwork and he looked up and smiled.

"It's always a pleasure to see you, come on in. You just caught me." He leaned back in his chair and ran his hands through his hair. "What's up?"

Annie sat in the chair opposite his desk and pulled the last two books from her bag, setting them in front of Tyler.

He leaned forward, opening both books and reading the messages. He found his paper with the four original messages and asked Annie to add the new ones.

Annie, Oliver knows what happened
Annie, check the trash
Annie, you need to do some real digging
Annie, it's not what it seems

She added:

Annie, you're getting closer. Don't give up
Annie, be careful who you talk to

Tyler read through the list. "Any ideas?"

"Well, no ideas on the messages, but I have a good idea who sent them."

Tyler's forehead wrinkled. "Oh?"

"Jillian. But I didn't have a chance to ask her any questions about them." Annie stood up. "Are you and JC going to the fireworks tonight?"

Tyler smiled. "Of course. And Dylan too. He's beside himself with excitement. See you there?"

"You bet. I have a date with Uncle Sam."

Tyler's face twisted in confusion.

"Jason," Annie clarified as she left his office.

JC had a rare moment of quiet when Annie walked to the front of the police station. "Enjoy the fireworks tonight. I hear Dylan can't wait."

JC beamed with happiness. "He's a new kid ever since Tyler took him fishing. It's all he talks about. Well, that and the fireworks, but tomorrow he'll be back on the fishing kick."

"How about you? Don't you go fishing with them?"

"Are you kidding? I like that time to myself. Let's me catch up on baking and cleaning and I always sneak in a few chapters of my favorite book."

Annie waved. "See you tonight."

She had debated with herself about showing the photo with the image of a woman to Tyler when she was in his office, but it was too blurry to be sure who it was. Without a positive identification, she decided it pointless to show him. She wanted to get more information first.

Annie and Roxy drove to Hazel's house. Was it Hazel in that photo?

Zoe barked when she pulled in. She already acted as if she was protecting her territory. When Roxy jumped out the back door of the car, the two dogs took off in a happy game of dog tag around the yard.

The commotion was enough to bring Hazel out of the house. "Checking up on me again?" she asked but without sounding upset.

Annie laughed, trying to dispel her own anxiety and wondering what the best way was to ask about the person in the photograph. No point in beating around the bush.

"No, I'm here about something else. I have a couple of questions." Annie carried her camera to Hazel who stood on her front step. "Take a look at this."

Hazel studied the photo.

"I took this before I found Peter unconscious in his blackberry field. Is it you?"

"No." She looked toward Peter's field.

"But you know who it is, don't you?"

Hazel filled her lungs and exhaled slowly. "It looks like Jillian. What was she doing there?"

"Can I come in? I have something else to talk to you about."

Hazel led the way to the bright kitchen and put the tea kettle on. She moved around quietly, taking cups from the cupboard, adding an assortment of tea bags and a container of honey to a tray. When the kettle whistled, she poured the hot water and brought the tray to the table.

"I started a new book. The main character is a therapy dog. This will be different from anything I've written before. The dog is going to help his owner solve the murders, and at the same time help someone else find the strength to move on with their life. Do you think anyone will want to read it?"

"Definitely. It sounds like a scenario that many people will be able to relate to. I'd like to buy the first copy." Annie realized the book was most likely about Hazel moving on with her own life.

Hazel smiled.

Annie blew on her tea before taking a tiny sip. "I've received several, six to be exact, messages printed inside books. One of them was in one of your books." She kept her eyes on Hazel's face.

Hazel blinked her intense blue eyes and pinched her lips together. "Can I see it?"

"No. I left them with the police. Well, the last four are at the police station, the first two were stolen from my bag." She paused to let Hazel digest that piece of information. "Do you know an Oliver?" Annie asked.

"This is Oliver." Hazel stroked the orange tabby cat curled in her lap.

"A cat?"

"Oliver is Jillian's cat but he is happy to hang out with me as his second choice. Why?"

Annie stood up and watched Roxy and Zoe through the kitchen window. They both were stretched out in the shade of an old apple tree. They must have tired each other out.

"The first message said *Oliver knows what happened*. Does that make any sense to you?"

"Not really. Oliver sometimes follows Jillian if she walks in the woods, but he never goes too far. Even if he knows something, how would he tell anyone?"

"Good point. Would he follow anyone besides Jillian?"

Hazel considered the question before answering. "Maybe."

"When I found Peter unconscious, there was an orange tabby cat meowing in the blackberry bushes near him. I think it was Oliver. Peter had been at your house. Do you think Oliver would have followed Peter? Or did Jillian follow Peter and Oliver followed her?"

Hazel stood up and Oliver fled from the kitchen. "What are you getting at?"

"I don't know, but I want to dig around where Peter fell. It didn't occur to me before, but he may have buried something before he passed out. Do you have a shovel I can borrow?"

Hazel led Annie to her shed and handed her a shovel. "I'm coming with you."

The dogs jumped up from their nap and ran ahead into the blackberry field. Annie hoped she could remember the exact spot since every row looked alike. Roxy ran down one row and Annie decided to follow her, hoping she was following a familiar trail.

Annie studied the bushes and stopped at the one with fertilizer spread underneath. Sticking the shovel in, she dug in several places but only managed to disturb the fertilizer and stir up the bad smell.

Hazel covered her nose. "What are you looking for?"

Annie leaned on the shovel. "One of the messages said to check the trash, but there were no clues in your trash so I thought it might mean to figure out what *should* have been in the trash but wasn't."

"You should write mysteries, I'm lost on this train of thought."

Annie scooped up dirt in a few more spots, carefully dumping the soil and poking around for something that shouldn't be there. Zoe joined in the fun and started digging with her paws. Annie bent over to push her out of the way but the glint of something just below the surface caught her eye.

Carefully, Annie used her fingers to move the soil until an insulin vial was uncovered. She poked around some more and found a second vial.

Hazel's eyes were as big as saucers and her hand covered her mouth. "Two vials. I gave him his normal injection." She stared at Annie. "Who gave the second one? That would kill him. Did Peter take the vials and bury them?"

"That might be the explanation. I'm going to find him and ask some questions."

Hazel grabbed Annie's arm. "Is that safe?"

"I think so." But to herself she said, I hope so.

Chapter 20

Annie walked to Peter's house with Roxy while Hazel took Zoe back to her house. With every step closer, Annie's heart beat faster and a feeling of dread settled in the pit of her stomach. What was she doing?

Before she could change her mind, a friendly voice called out to her.

"Annie, what brings you and Roxy this way?"

She saw Peter waving with Logan and Ariel tagging along behind.

He wouldn't dare do anything in front of his grandkids, Annie decided, and felt some of her tense muscles relax slightly.

Bandit darted from behind the kids, streaking toward Roxy in pure puppy happiness.

"You picked out a winner for the kids. Bandit is a smart one." Peter chuckled with delight as the kids followed the two dogs, creating a blur of legs and arms. "So, what can I do for you?" He swiveled his head around. "How did you get here? I don't see your car."

"I had a few questions for Hazel and I walked from her house. Are you taking a walk? Could I join you?"

"Of course. Maybe Bandit will show you her clever trick."

"She already knows a trick? You've only had her for a few hours."

"Yeah. She loves it here. She already figured how delicious the blackberries are and can pick her own. I hope she doesn't eat too many and get sick."

Peter stopped and let the kids run around with the two dogs before deciding which row to lead everyone down.

They walked in a comfortable silence, giving Annie time to organize her thoughts and her questions for Peter. Kirk's words about Peter's anger about the land sale, rang in her ears. Just because she never saw that side of his behavior didn't mean he wasn't capable of violence. She had to be careful.

With her camera as a link to one of her questions, she snapped shots of the kids, dogs and Peter. Finally, once the kids slowed to a walk, Annie asked Peter to stand with the two kids in front of a blackberry bush loaded with berries for a family portrait. She snapped several times to be sure at least one photo would capture everyone with their eyes open and natural smiles on their faces.

"Can we see the picture?" Ariel and Logan shouted as soon as Annie released them from the pose.

She crouched down with one knee on the ground and scrolled through the last few photos. They both decided they liked the same one, and Annie had to admit, it was the best one of the lot. Standing, she let Peter view the screen.

"Can you make a copy for me? I'm trying to convince Emily to move here so the kids can get out of the cramped apartment she has and have all this to enjoy." His arm swooped around to take in all the rows and rows of berry bushes.

"I'd be happy to." Annie scrolled to the photo from the day she found Peter unconscious. "Here's another photo I'd like you to take a look at."

He stared at the blurry figure, moving his head closer as if that would make the image come into focus. "Who is that?"

"I hoped you could tell me. I took this photo before I found you unconscious and I just discovered the figure in this shot. Maybe this person can shed some light on what happened that morning."

Peter straightened and stepped away from Annie. "What do you mean? Shed light on what?"

Annie sighed and walked toward Peter. "Who killed Robbie." She reached into her pocket and showed him the insulin vials in her hand. "I found these buried near the bush where you passed out the other day."

He leaned closer and shrugged his shoulders. "That's odd and ridiculous. How could you remember which bush it was?"

"The smell isn't so bad anymore, but it's still there. Hazel's dog dug these up. Robbie died from an overdose of insulin. How did these end up under your blackberry bushes?" Annie studied Peter's face.

The color drained from tan to pale. "I have no idea."

She knew he was lying. He acted like a little boy who got caught with his hand in the cookie jar with cookie crumbs around his mouth but insisted he never took a cookie. "Peter, who are you protecting?"

He gazed over his fields and stuck his hands in the pockets of his pants.

"You went back into the house after Luke left, didn't you?"

"Why would I do that?"

Annie patted his arm. "Maybe you need to tell me why. Luke saw you with Jillian at the side of the house and he saw you go back inside."

Peter's shoulders sagged, suddenly adding ten years to his age. "Come on kids, we should be getting back to the house. Your mother will be wondering where we wandered off to." He turned toward Annie. "They had such a good time in the parade, but Emily thought they should have a break here before we head back for the fireworks tonight. I'll bring them inside and then we can talk."

As they all walked back to the house, Annie sent a text to Jason telling him where she was, just in case. What did she think Peter might do to her? A shiver traveled through her body. Better not to think about that.

Annie waited outside in the shade with Roxy and Bandit. Peter returned with two tall glasses of ice cold lemonade and two bowls of blackberry ice cream.

"Emily was busy while I had the kids. She whipped up a batch of ice cream. It doesn't get much better than this," Peter said as he handed Annie a bowl.

He drained his glass and settled on the grass with his back against the tree. "Okay then, where were we?"

"Why did you go back inside Robbie's house?"

"Jillian was upset about the fact that Robbie wouldn't let her visit Hazel and she was tired of sneaking around. Actually, she was furious. She hated how Robbie bossed her mother around. I went back in for her, to find out if Luke got what he came for."

"What happened inside?"

"Robbie was sitting in his old ragged recliner. He must have had that dirty old thing for fifty years. I suppose Hazel tried to make him get rid of it, but he never listened to her." Peter tasted his ice cream before continuing. "His eyes were closed and I thought he was asleep. I noticed an insulin vial next to his chair, and when I moved closer, my foot knocked something under the table." He closed his eyes and leaned his head back.

Annie tried the ice cream. "You're right about this blackberry ice cream. It's the best I've ever had."

The sound of their spoons clicking on the bowl and the dogs panting next to them was all that disturbed the silence.

"What did your foot bump into?" Annie finally asked.

"Another insulin vial. I picked it up and put it on the table. I don't know why there were two."

Annie nodded. "He died from an insulin overdose. Why didn't you tell the police about this?"

"I panicked. When I looked closer at Robbie, his skin was gray. I didn't touch him, but I suspected he was dead. I grabbed the two vials and left as quickly as possible. Everyone knew I was against Robbie selling his land for a condo development. I never kept that opinion to myself. I was afraid I would be a suspect since my fingerprints would be on the vials if I left them there."

"Did you bury them under the blackberry bushes?"

"No. I don't know how they got there. I threw them in some weeds between Robbie's house and my land."

"Someone must have seen you and picked them up." Bandit had her nose in the empty ice cream bowls, licking up any leftover sweetness. "Someone picked out the perfect name for this little thief." Annie laughed as she shooed the puppy away. She picked up her camera again. "Take another look at the photo I showed you earlier and tell me who you think it is."

Annie held the camera for Peter while he studied the photo. "It's so blurry. I'm not sure, but if I had to make a guess, I would say it was Hazel. She's always walking in the woods with her cat. It's kind of creepy sometimes how she suddenly appears out of the blue."

Annie sat forward. "Her orange cat?"

"Yeah, that's the one. I found him in my barn when I came back from the hospital on Wednesday. I don't know how he got way over here."

Annie's phone vibrated in her pocket. A text from Jason read, *I'm home, want to meet me for dinner?*

She sent a quick message back, *On my way.*

Peter picked up the bowls and offered a hand to help Annie up. "I hope, for Jillian's sake, that Hazel didn't finally lose it and give Robbie an overdose."

"One more question, Peter." Annie waited until Peter met her eyes. "What's your relationship with Hazel? You seem to know a lot about her."

"It's complicated. She doesn't want anything to do with me, and I understand, but Jillian fills me in once in a while. I truly want Hazel to be happy, and as long as Robbie was alive, she wasn't going to ever move out of his ugly shadow."

"You think the last straw was Robbie selling the land? That might have made her give him an overdose?"

He shrugged. "Have you read any of her books? There's always a murder with a complicated trail of suspects."

"But why would she pick up the vials after you threw them away and bury them right where you passed out? She was with me when Zoe dug up the vials. She acted genuinely surprised."

"I can't answer that. If she murdered Robbie, she certainly has the imagination to leave a difficult trail to untangle. Maybe she was hoping to point the clues toward me. I wouldn't put it past her. She never forgave me for not marrying her when she got pregnant with Jillian."

Chapter 21

As Annie walked across the field to Hazel's house where she'd left her car, she wasn't sure if she believed everything Peter told her. He also had something to gain with Robbie dead: no condos in his backyard.

And what about Luke? He was with Robbie before Peter went in for the second time. Maybe he gave Robbie a second shot of insulin. How did Jillian fit into the whole picture? Bits and pieces continued to be revealed but the whole mystery was still just that, a mystery. And was everyone telling the truth? Annie doubted it.

The farmhouse was quiet, not even Zoe outside to greet her. Annie looked at her car but sighed and decided she should at least make sure Hazel was all right before leaving.

She poked her head inside the front door. Silence. Annie closed the door, happy to leave to meet Jason. Maybe Jillian picked her up and brought her into town for the fireworks.

She couldn't head straight home. Pulling into the police station, Annie dropped the insulin vials into a small shopping bag and brought them inside. JC smiled and put a finger up so Annie waited until she was off the phone.

"Can you give this to Tyler for me? I don't have time to talk now, but tell him I found these buried in Peter Hayworth's blackberry field."

JC's eyebrows shot up in surprise but took the bag and walked down the hall toward Tyler's office, giving Annie an opportunity to leave before Tyler had a chance to corner her.

Driving through Catfish Cove was stop and go with traffic, pedestrians and everyone from around the lake looking for a parking spot. Annie wasn't planning to drive back to town, she would walk or watch the fireworks from Jason's porch. She smiled to herself with that thought.

She hurried into her apartment, happy to see Smokey curled up on the window seat. He stretched and yawned before jumping down to stand next to his bowl. "You are so predictable." Annie told her black kitty as she gave him some food.

"How about you Roxy? You must be ready for some food too after your busy day." Annie poured food into Roxy's bowl and filled the water bowl with fresh clean water.

She stripped off her sweaty clothes and jumped into the shower. The water washed away more than dust and sweat. She let her tension go down the drain too. She told herself she wasn't going to think about Robbie anymore for the night. Someone else could put the pieces of that puzzle together.

Annie pulled on her favorite ivory capris and a soft blue cotton t-shirt. She automatically checked for her silver strawberry necklace around her neck. She loved the necklace that Jason had given her for Valentine's Day and seldom took it off.

Walking out the door with Roxy at her side, she crossed the driveway to Jason's house.

"I'm trying something new tonight." Annie heard Jason's voice coming from the front of the house.

She walked through the living room, across the porch and saw him trying to light a grill.

"You're cooking from scratch tonight?" she asked with a half grin.

"I'm grilling salmon. How hard can that be?" Jason said as he held the start button on the grill. Nothing happened.

"I thought you were a vegetarian?"

"Yeah, well, I eat fish occasionally."

Annie laughed out loud. "Jason. You don't have the gas tank hooked up to the grill. Here, let me help."

Jason stood back and watched as Annie hooked the hose from the grill to the gas tank and got the grill preheating.

"See," he said, "how hard can it be? Especially if someone else does it." He pulled her into his arms and gave her a tight hug before she could squirm away and swat him for his deception.

"I promise I'll make a super salad if you cook the salmon," he said as he gave her a pathetic look. "And dessert too."

Annie attempted an annoyed sigh but a laugh escape instead. She was happy to help with the cooking. Maybe someday Jason would expand his ability in the food department, but making amazing salads was an admirable start indeed.

"Helloooo? Where is everyone?" a familiar voice called from inside the house.

Annie shot Jason a puzzled look. "Why is Leona here?"

"Remember how I said I'd supply dessert too? Actually, Leona is bringing dessert."

Annie tried to feel happy but Leona could be so overpowering and she had been looking forward to relaxing with Jason. Alone.

"And, maybe I forgot to mention—"

Annie cut him off. "More people?"

Jason nodded. "It's so crowded in town, I invited a few people to join us to watch the fireworks here. It is one of the best viewing spots away from the crowds."

Before he could explain more, Leona and Danny appeared on the porch. "Where do you want me to put the dessert?" She held out a cheesecake covered with strawberries, blueberries, dollops of cream spaced around the edge and shaved chocolate sprinkled in the center.

Annie's mood thawed a bit seeing the mouthwatering dessert. "It's beautiful, Leona, and red, white and blue for the Fourth of July. That would have sold well in the café this weekend."

"I made several and they did fly off the shelf. I had to hide this one or I would have come empty handed."

Danny handed Jason a bottle of blackberry wine. "This is my contribution. I can't cook to save my life."

Leona gave him a shocked look. "Is that all I am to you? Your meal ticket?"

Danny sputtered and his face turned a deep shade of red. "Of course not."

Leona laughed her deep-from-the-belly laugh and hugged Danny. "Loosen up. I'm just teasing."

Watching their interaction, Annie saw the genuine affection Leona had for Danny. Maybe this romance would turn out differently for her. They both had been hurt in the past and put up artificial defenses for protection. Danny's kind nature would soften Leona's coarse edges and Leona's zest for life might pull Danny far away from his war demons and drinking.

Annie felt a nudge. "Lost in a deep thought?" Jason asked.

She smiled at him. "Leona and Danny make a good couple. And I can't wait to taste that cheesecake."

"There's something I can't wait to taste," he said in a throaty whisper as he leaned in and kissed her tenderly. "Yum. Even better than I imagined. I wouldn't mind seconds of that."

The sound of someone clearing his throat made both Annie and Jason turn suddenly.

Tyler stood awkwardly, fidgeting with a bag in his hand. "Annie. Can I talk to you for a minute? It's important."

Jason scowled, obviously annoyed that Annie's ex-fiancé intruded on their private moment.

"Yes, of course," Annie answered. She knew exactly what was in the bag but had hoped this conversation could have waited until the next day.

"JC gave me these as soon as you dropped this off at the police station. Where did you find these insulin vials?"

Annie recounted the details of her visit with Hazel and Peter. "Honestly, I don't know what to believe. Everyone keeps pointing fingers at someone else. And what about Luke?"

Tyler held Annie's arm. "Why did you go there by yourself? Someone murdered Robbie, and if you poke around in the wrong place you could be next."

"There's something else I guess I should show you. It's in my apartment." Annie led Tyler up the stairs and picked up her camera. "I was finally going through all the photos I took since last Wednesday, and found this."

Tyler squinted and studied the blurry image. "Who is this?"

"I'm not sure. That's why I went to talk to Hazel. I took this photo on Wednesday before I found Peter unconscious. I thought the person in this photo might know something."

"And?"

"Hazel said it might be Jillian but Peter thought it looked like Hazel. He said Hazel walks in the woods a lot with her cat."

Tyler still looked confused.

"I saw an orange cat in the blackberry bush where I found Peter. Hazel must have been there with her cat. I think she followed Peter after he was in the house with Robbie and she buried the vials to make it look like he murdered Robbie."

"Or Peter killed Robbie and he buried the vials before he passed out. Or these could be old vials that aren't even connected to the day Robbie died. Wouldn't that make more sense?" Tyler asked.

Annie paced around the room. "That's the problem. I don't know what makes sense anymore. No one liked Robbie. Peter, Hazel and Luke all had a reason to want him dead and they were all at the house at the right time. I'm not sure how Jillian fits in the picture. Hazel told me she gave Robbie his insulin shot like she always did. Why would she kill him that day and not some other day? For that matter, why would someone *ever* kill someone else?" Annie asked in frustration. "How can we understand the mind of a killer if it's something we would never do?"

"I'm worried about you, Annie. If you uncovered clues to Robbie's murder and the killer knows you're on to them, you could be a target. And one more thing," he added. "Luke stopped at the police station earlier and told me he was leaving town, giving up on getting the land. I thought it was a bit strange, as if he wanted an alibi or something. Don't do anything foolish. Okay?"

Annie waved her hand dismissively. "I'm not a fool."

She opened the door and waited for Tyler to walk out before closing the door and following him down the stairs. "I thought you didn't have to work tonight?"

"I'll be at the fireworks. Keeping my eyes open."

Music drifted from Jason's living room, drowning out her frustration from the day. Was she looking at the information completely wrong? It was too easy to get one idea and not see other pathways. Did Luke somehow figure out an angle to get Hazel to sell her land? She shook the thoughts away, determined to have a romantic evening with Jason.

Her phone rang. She paused at the bottom of her stairs, willing herself to ignore the ringing phone. The music, the smell of food grilling, the sound of laughter all pulled her toward Jason's house.

Until she couldn't ignore the ring and she heard Hazel's frantic voice.

Chapter 22

"Slow down. You aren't making any sense," Annie said slowly, trying to calm Hazel.

Silence. Annie was afraid Hazel hung up but then she heard a big intake of air.

"Jillian is in trouble. Can you help me?"

Annie looked at Jason's house. Everything she wanted was right in front of her but Hazel's voice sounded so desperate. "Where are you?"

"I'm at the café. Jillian gave me a ride to town and told me she had something important to do so I did some people watching. We were supposed to meet up again at the cafe but she never showed up."

"Okay," Annie said as she started to walk to her car. "How do you know she's in trouble?"

"Just come. Please." The phone went dead.

Annie slid into her car and threw her phone on the seat. This wasn't foolish, was it? With so many people in town, what could go wrong? Hazel was probably just overreacting to something and Annie would be back at Jason's house before anyone missed her.

Ten minutes later, Annie saw Hazel pacing in the parking lot behind the Cove's Corner building. Annie stopped next to Hazel and told her to get in since the parking lot was so full there wasn't even room for a bicycle.

"Thank you for coming. I didn't know who else to call."

"What's going on? You said Jillian is in trouble."

"She called me and said she was with Luke. He's trying to convince Jillian to get me to sell the land."

Annie drove slowly, looking for a parking spot even though she knew all spots had been taken ages ago. "Where are they?"

"That's what got me worried. As soon as I asked her, the phone went dead."

"Maybe she was in a dead spot. I think you're overreacting."

Zoe sat on Hazel's lap with her head hanging out the window and her ears flapping in the wind as they drove.

"I'm taking you home. Maybe Jillian will go there when she can't find you in town."

They drove in silence but Annie was fuming inside. Why did she answer that phone call? This wasn't her problem and she didn't want to be part of it.

A black Lexus sped down the road almost forcing Annie's car into the ditch. Something was familiar about the car but she was so angry with Hazel her brain couldn't sort out what it was. She slowed down as she approached Hazel's driveway.

"Stop," Hazel blurted out.

What now, Annie thought as she clenched her jaw, but she pulled into the driveway and stopped.

Without any explanation, Hazel jumped out and ran to her mailbox. That's when Annie noticed the flap was open and a book was sticking partly out.

The car, she realized, was Luke Carbone's. What was he doing here? Looking for Hazel? Tyler said he had left town.

Hazel stood, staring at the inside of the book. Annie looked over her shoulder.

Stay in your house and wait for instructions. Don't call the police.

The words were printed in black ink, slanted left. Not the same writing in the messages Annie received.

Hazel stared at Annie with tears ready to spill over the corner of her eyes. "I knew it. Jillian is in trouble. When Robbie wouldn't let me see or call Jillian, this was our secret way to communicate. She must have told Luke how to get in touch with me."

"Get in the car. I'll take you to your house, then I'm going to the police."

Hazel grabbed her arm, her eyes wild. "You can't do that. Didn't you read the message? It says not to call the police. I'll wait at the house and you can leave if you want to."

That was the best advice Annie heard in the last half hour, but how could she leave Hazel alone? She would wait until the next message came, then reassess her options.

Once inside, they didn't have to wait long. The back door opened and Jillian burst into the house, out of breath. She had bits of leaves and twigs sticking in her hair.

Hazel hugged her. "Are you all right?"

Jillian slumped into a kitchen chair. "Luke told me he wanted to talk about the land, but when I got in his car, he locked the doors and wouldn't let me out. He stopped to make a phone call and I jumped out his door and ran into the woods. He started to follow me but I knew he would never have a chance. I know the woods too well."

Annie stood up. "Maybe we should call the police now. They'll be able to catch him before he gets too far away."

"I already did that. Tyler said to wait here."

Annie sighed. What a mess. She was missing grilled salmon, salad and blackberry wine for someone else's drama.

Hazel put the tea kettle on.

Jillian opened the refrigerator. "There's still some blackberry pie in here. Who wants a piece?"

Annie said, "No thanks." She was saving any appetite for Leona's red, white and blue cheesecake. They better save her some or she was going to be in a supremely bad mood.

Jillian got out plates and cut three pieces anyway. From Annie's seat, she could see Jillian pour some fresh berries on two of the pieces.

Hazel carried the tea kettle, herbal teas and three cups to the table, sitting next to her daughter.

"I'm glad you're safe. I was frantic when you didn't meet me in town."

Jillian nodded. "Good thing you called Annie, she always knows what to do."

Jillian placed the two pieces of pie with fresh berries in front of Annie and Hazel, keeping the plain pie for herself.

"Where did you get the fresh blueberries, Jillian?" Annie asked, her hairs sticking up on her neck.

"Just a lucky find as I was walking through the fields. I don't think Peter will notice a few missing blueberries."

Hazel dug in with her fork, but before the pie made it to her mouth, Annie knocked the bite of pie away. "Don't eat it. Blueberries aren't in season for another month, are they?" Annie kept her eyes focused on Jillian's face.

Jillian smirked. "You've been reading too many mysteries, Annie. Go ahead, enjoy the delicious pie."

Hazel looked from Jillian to Annie. "What's going on?"

"Your daughter is trying to poison us. All the clues she sent me, pointing suspicion to everyone but herself." Every jumbled bit of the mystery clicked into place in Annie's brain. "It was you all along, wasn't it, Jillian? You have a back way to the house. The way through the woods so Robbie wouldn't know you were here."

Jillian smiled, so proud of herself. "Robbie was scared when I walked into the room after Mom gave him his insulin injection. He tried to protect himself by banning me from the house because he knew I wanted him dead, but I was patient. Everything fell into place on Wednesday. Mom gave Robbie his shot and was supposed to take a walk to meet me behind Peter's fields." She looked at her mother.

Annie was riveted to her seat, wanting to flee but needing to find out what happened. Hazel sat with her mouth open, in shock at what she was hearing.

"I had to hide in the closet because you were still in the house and you heard Peter arguing with Robbie. That was a bonus. When Peter left, slamming the door, I had just enough time to give him another injection before Luke showed up. His speech was confused enough that no one would understand what he was saying. Then Luke arrived. I made sure to catch Peter outside and convince him to go back in to ask Robbie if he signed the papers. I thought Peter would see that Robbie was dead and would call the police. Luke would be blamed, but Peter didn't make that call and he found the extra insulin vial."

Hazel kept blinking her eyes, staring at her daughter in disbelief. "You buried the vials near Peter? I thought he did it."

"I had to figure out another plan, and having Peter take the blame was almost as good as pinning it on Luke." She ate a piece of her pie. "I got the ideas from your books, Mom. Always point the blame to someone you don't like. Peter hurt you and I wanted him to suffer."

"But that's fiction. It doesn't work like that in real life." Hazel looked at the phone hanging on the kitchen wall. "You didn't really call the police, did you?"

Jillian smiled.

Annie's heart fell into her stomach.

"No one is coming. Luke is walking to town which will take him a long time. His fancy leather shoes are sure to give him blisters." Jillian pushed the pie plates closer to Annie and Hazel. "So, go ahead, enjoy the pie. I have to figure out a new ending to the story. This wasn't part of the original plot but I'll come up with something." She continued to eat her piece of pie.

Annie thought about making a dash for her car. She could picture exactly where her phone was. If she could get to it before Jillian stopped her . . .

"I know what you're thinking, Annie." Jillian reached into her pocket and pulled out Annie's phone. "Just enjoy your last few minutes."

Chapter 23

Tires crunched on the driveway, breaking the silence. Jillian ran to the window, giving Annie an opening to run.

Outside, Annie hoped to see a friendly face. It was Peter's car with Luke sitting next to him. Annie felt her blood run cold. Nothing made sense. Was she still in danger? Before any words were spoken, a siren cut through the darkening sky.

Tyler's car screeched to a dusty stop with Jason's car right behind.

Annie stood frozen, her brain unable to make her muscles move.

Tyler took one look at Annie and asked, "Where is she?"

"Inside."

Peter took both of Annie's arms. "Are you all right?"

"I don't know. Why is Luke with you?"

"Jillian stole his car and I found him walking to town. It's a miracle I decided to stop. Don't worry, he's not going to hurt you."

Annie finally felt herself breathing again. In, out. The motion helped to calm her nerves. Jason was at her side, wrapping his arms around her. "I thought I would never see you again when you didn't come back. I thought you ran off with Tyler."

Annie laughed. "That's what you thought? You never considered that I had been kidnapped by a psycho killer?"

"Is that what happened?"

"Well, not exactly. I went willingly. Foolishly." She sagged against Jason's strong body, inhaling the delicious scent of food. "Did you save any for me?"

He stood back to look into Annie's face. "Any what?"

"Cheesecake."

Jason laughed. A beautiful, deep, satisfied laugh. "If you're thinking about food, I know you'll be fine."

Tyler came outside with Hazel. "Jillian got away."

Hazel looked like her whole world had crashed in on her. She sighed. "I know where she'll be. We had a secret meeting spot in the woods."

***

Jason brought Annie back to Cobblestone Cottage. Of course, Leona and Danny were still there, and once Mia heard about the drama, she was waiting for Annie too. Roxy ran in circles of excitement before sniffing Annie from head to foot until she was satisfied that all was well with her person.

Jason poured Annie a glass of the blackberry wine and made her sit on the swing on the porch. Once she was comfortable with Roxy leaning against her legs, he brought a big piece of Leona's cheesecake.

"Since you didn't have any dinner, you get a super-sized slice. Do you want extra berries on top?"

"Not blueberries." She shuddered at the thought of Jillian's attempt to poison Annie and Hazel.

Jason settled down next to Annie as she sipped her wine and enjoyed the cheesecake. He put his arm around her shoulders and pulled her close.

"I really was in a panic when you didn't come back and we discovered your car gone. I couldn't have been happier when I saw you standing outside Hazel's house in one piece," he whispered in her ear, sending goosebumps up and down her neck.

Suddenly, the sky burst with colors. The crowd in the center of town gasped as one and the sound carried across the water.

Annie relaxed completely into Jason's strong arms and sighed contentedly. "All's well that ends well, right?"

Jason kissed her.

Behind the scenes with Lyndsey

When I was younger—yes, many years ago—blackberries were never my favorite fruit because of the incredible thorns they have. Picking them was painful. Several years ago, some brilliant plant breeder figured out how to breed a thornless, or prickle-free, blackberry. Now, blackberries are special. You don't usually see them for sale, so if you don't grow them yourself, you won't know their unique flavor.

So, when July comes around, and my grandsons are visiting, we trek out to the blackberry patch to enjoy the juicy fruit. If I get behind on pruning the blackberry canes, it becomes a tangled jungle and the boys always find something special besides the berries hiding in the snarled canes. The most exciting discovery is when we spy a bird's nest tucked in the brambles. The boys have learned to be respectful of the nest, but if it's low enough, I pick them up so they can see the eggs. The most common nest we find is a sparrow nest with several pale blue eggs spotted with brown. Sometimes, we are even rewarded by seeing the baby birds with their yellow beaks raised hoping for a meal. I tell the boys that Momma Bird is nearby waiting for us to leave so she can get back to her job.

Once our containers are filled, we go back inside to make our BlackBuried Pie.

Mark and Danny climb on the chairs at the kitchen island knowing they're in for one of Mimi's treats. It's hard to beat the chocolate covered strawberries they love, but making their own mini pies is probably their second favorite treat.

The first step is to have a cool drink before we start. After we finish our lemonade, of course it's time for a bathroom break, a good hand scrub and then it's back to work.

I have to admit that after years of making pie crusts from scratch using my mother's recipe, I've gotten a bit lazy and I use premade crusts. So, whatever your choice is, make sure to use the best ingredients and use your own crust recipe or cheat like I do and take a short cut with a premade crust.

I put my favorite pie dish, the one my father made when he was still able to make pottery, on the island. I cut one pie crust in half and give each boy one piece. They sprinkle some sugar and berries on one side and fold the other side over the filling. The part they like the best is pressing their little thumbs along the edge of the crust to seal in the fruit. They sprinkle a bit more sugar on top and I slide their creations onto a pan.

While they are busy with their mini pies, I put my pie together. First, I preheat the oven to 425 degrees F. After I line the 9" pie dish with my store bought crust, I brush beaten egg over the crust which helps to keep it from getting soggy.

Setting that aside, I get the filling ready. I combine 4 cups of fresh blackberries with ½ cup flour and ½ cup white sugar and spoon that into the prepared crust. Next, I spread another cup of blackberries on top of the sweetened berries. Finally, I squeeze half of a lemon and sprinkle two tablespoons of chopped butter over the berries.

I cover the berries with the second pie crust and crimp the edges to seal in all the deliciousness. I brush the top with a little more egg and sprinkle another one or two teaspoons of sugar on top.

The last step before popping everything into the oven is to poke vent holes in the crust. In my house, this is very important! My pie gets a big 'B'. My husband wandered in and I had to explain to him that the 'B' is for blackberry. Danny's mini pie gets a 'D' and Mark's mini pie gets an 'M'. They are always worried their pies will get mixed up, but once I put the letters on, they're all smiles again.

Bake the pie in the preheated oven for 15 minutes, then reduce the temperature to 375 degrees F and bake for another 20 to 25 minutes, or until the filling is bubbly and the crust is a beautiful golden brown. The smaller pies take less time depending on how much fruit the boys put inside, so I keep an eye on them and take them out as soon as the crust is golden.

After the pies cool down, it's snack time and we sit in the shade of my flower garden enjoying BlackBuried Pie and vanilla ice cream. What could be better on a hot July day?

~Lyndsey

ABOUT THE AUTHOR

Lyndsey Cole lives in New England in a small rural town with her husband, dogs, cats and chickens. She has plenty of space to grow lots of beautiful perennials. Sitting in the garden with the scent of lilac, peonies, lily of the valley or whatever is in bloom, stimulates her imagination about mysteries and romance.

ONE LAST THING . . .

If you enjoyed this installment of The Black Cat Café Cozy Mystery Series, be sure to join my FREE COZY MYSTERY BOOK CLUB! Be in the know for new releases, promotions, sales, and the possibility to receive advanced reader copies. Join the club here—
http://LyndseyColeBooks.com

OTHER BOOKS BY LYNDSEY COLE

The Black Cat Café Series

BlueBuried Muffins

Annie Fisher is scared. She's scared of the mess her boyfriend, Max Parker, is in the middle of and she has to get out of his house. She puts a whole state between them and drives like a madwoman from Cooper, NY to her hometown of Catfish Cove, NH where she hopes she'll be safe.

She decides to start a new life, a life she ran away from two years ago but is finding herself missing as soon as she gets home. Annie immediately has a place to live, a job at her Aunt Leona's new café— Black Cat Café—and plenty of boyfriend prospects. Unfortunately, she also has plenty of bad things follow her.

Like Max Parker. Only the next time she sees him he's dead. Suddenly everyone she runs into turns into a potential suspect. There are ghosts from her past and new neighbors that make her hair stand on end. And right in the middle of everything is Annie with Max's last warning to her—Don't trust anyone. Will those words prove to keep her safe or put too much distance between Annie and those trying to help her?

StrawBuried in Chocolate

Annie Fisher wakes up on Friday the thirteenth, but she reminds herself she's not superstitious. The Black Cat Café is loaded up with special Valentine's Day goodies, the most popular being Annie's chocolate covered strawberries. She is so looking forward to a romantic weekend with current flame, landlord and neighbor, Jason Hunter.

But when her Aunt Leona finds a body in Jason's house, all plans for that romantic weekend are scrapped. All Annie, Leona, Mia and Jason can think about is who killed Lacy McGuire and why.

With more and more clues pointing toward Leona as the killer, they need to work fast to figure out who the real killer is before Leona ends up in jail for good. To complicate matters for Annie, information surfaces about her birth parents, a mystery she's been working on for the past few years. She thinks she wants to find the answers, but will it destroy her world?

Now, Annie must struggle to save her aunt, but as she questions neighbors and relatives, will she put herself in danger with the real killer? Will she save her aunt but get herself killed in the process?

The Lily Bloom Series

Begonias Mean Beware

Misty Valley has a new flower shop in town, and as soon as Lily Bloom hangs the open sign, she lands the biggest wedding in town. Plus, the handsome new guy moves in right next door to Lily. She's well on her way to a successful and exciting season.

But when the groom is found dead in her kitchen just days before he's supposed to be walking down the aisle, Lily has to arrange the trail of flowers to try to solve the mystery. With the help of her scooter-riding, pot-smoking mother, Iris, her sister, Daisy, and her dog, Rosie, Lily races from one disaster to another, all the while keeping herself out of the killer's sight.

Will she solve the cascade of events in time or get caught by the criminals running illegal gambling and selling drugs in Misty Valley? Will romance blossom between Lily and her new neighbor?

Queen of Poison

Business at Lily's Beautiful Blooms Flower Shop is growing like weeds after a rainstorm. She's been asked to do the main flower arrangement for the Arts in Bloom opening at the Misty Valley Museum. Everything seems to be coming up rosy and she's even falling head over heels for the man of her dreams, Ryan Steele, her neighbor and the police chief of Misty Valley.

Until she sees a sleek red convertible drive into his driveway. And an even sleeker red head climbs out of the car. She thought that was all she had to deal with until the founder of the museum drops dead in her arms and another body has all fingers pointing toward Lily.

With help from her mom, Iris, her sister, Daisy and their friends Marigold and Tamara, Lily tries to arrange the clues to point to the real killer. Can she sort it out in time before a third body—maybe hers—ends up in the morgue? Can she get her romance growing again with the handsome police chief of Misty Valley? Or will she be left to sort through the clues alone?

Roses are Dead

Business is popping for Lily as wedding season is in full swing. The brides are all over the place from easy-to-please to last-minute-panics. But one in particular stands out—a leggy brunette who is looking for plenty of red roses for her wedding to Police Chief Ryan Steele.

Lily is beside herself with betrayal that Ryan would lead her on like that, all the while engaged to this beauty. It's almost too much to take until the bride is found dead, surrounded by none other than the very roses she'd been admiring.

Lily shoots to the top of the suspect list, a place she's been all too often lately. And as she starts to uncover more about the woman's past, she's thrown into another game of cat and mouse. Only she's not sure if she's the cat or the mouse. Will she be able to follow the clues to the real killer in time? Or is everyone connected to Ryan Steele in danger and Lily could be next?

Drowning in Dahlias

The business is heating up at Beautiful Blooms and Lily's flower arrangements can be found all over Misty Valley at any type of event. And to add to the chaos, she's lost the full time help of her sister, Daisy, who has started a specialty cake making business on the side. Together, they make the perfect team, especially when wealthy estate owner, Walter Nash, enlists both of them to cater and decorate for the 55th birthday party for his wife.

But when they show up with their deliveries and find the love of his life, Harriet Nash, dead on the floor, the dynamic duo is suddenly threatened. With a house full of family and friends to celebrate her birthday, there are too many suspects to keep straight.

Lily's biggest challenge now is to find the killer before the killer finds her. But without a murder weapon at the crime scene, the questions continue to pile up without any answers. Who would have wanted Harriet dead the most? She had plenty of money, but would someone have been so greedy? As Lily and Daisy get closer to solving the murder, things take a turn for the worse with a threat on Lily's life.

Hidden by the Hydrangeas

Lily Bloom can't seem to keep her thoughts away from marriage. Maybe it's just because her mom tied the knot with her childhood sweetheart Walter Nash, but it's gotten Lily thinking about her own relationship with Ryan Steele and if it's going anywhere.

But those thoughts are quickly replaced with who is carrying a dead body, and who that dead body might be. The only thing Lily knows is that she's been spotted by the killer so she has to hope this mystery is solved before she's the next one in a body bag.

When Walter's best friend turns up as the likeliest suspect, Lily's mom is beside herself with worry and convinces Lily that she's the best person to solve this case. But suspects keep piling up with not quite enough evidence to prove anything. Will Lily be able to put all the pieces together before the killer sniffs out her trail?

Christmas Tree Catastrophe

Lily Bloom couldn't be more excited for Christmas Eve when she will say "I do" to the man she loves. She just has the library opening to get through and then all the town's focus will be on her.

But things start going wrong almost from the very first moment she's getting setup for the library's event. Not only is there plenty of disagreement among those helping, but one of the co-chairs who is in charge of the whole event winds up dead the day before the ceremony.

With everyone who was helping setup under a microscope, Lily is in a race against time to be able to get married. When one of her best friends winds up in jail for the murder Lily knows she didn't commit, the pressure's on to find the real murderer.

Will Lily be able to prove her friend's innocence? Or will she find herself in even more trouble and face a wedding in a jail cell or the hospital? Or worse—will there be no wedding at all because the bride is the new target?

Printed in the USA
CPSIA information can be obtained
at www.ICGtesting.com
LVHW041003170124
769088LV00008BA/341